T0169531

"Brilliant evocation of *el otro México*, 'the other Mexico,' by the writer whose inspiration underlies Gabriel García Márquez's *One Hundred Years of Solitude*."
—*Kirkus Reviews*, starred review

"Rulfo's memorable images…help to fill out the oeuvre of an important Mexican writer."
—*Publishers Weekly*

"Rulfo, through his photographs and his books, seems to be saying, Look! See! This world is here before us, it lacerates us with the anguished and ill-fated weight of its tangible reality. Come look!"
—EDUARDO RIVERO, author of *Juan Rulfo's Mexico*

"Far from the simple imitative realism of earlier Latin American novels, his essentialist work is on the level of myth and archetype."
—ROCKWELL GRAY, *The Chicago Tribune*

"Rulfo's work is at its core about people who do their best to unburden themselves of the stories they never stop telling."
—PETER ORNER, *The Rumpus*

"[*Pedro Páramo* is] a tale that is firmly rooted in its own culture yet so fundamentally human in its focus that it speaks across cultural borders."
—*Publishers Weekly*

"One of the most influential of the century's books…[I]t would be hard to overestimate its impact on literature in Spanish in the last forty years."
—SUSAN SONTAG, author of *The Benefactor*

"The work of Juan Rulfo is not only the highest expression which the Mexican novel has attained until now: through *Pedro Páramo* we can find the thread that leads us to the new Latin American novel."
—CARLOS FUENTES, author of *La muerte de Artemio Cruz* (*The Death of Artemio Cruz*)

"What is fascinating about Rulfo…is that in one single time frame, he lets the dead and the living coincide. Have conversations."
—VALERIA LUISELLI, author of *The Story of My Teeth*

"His is a text in which meaning is subsumed into an architecture of shadows and whispers, and into the ebb and flow of the vernacular."
—SUHAYL SAADI, *The Independent*

"[Rulfo's] work is built on an intricate lattice of time and space, but it doesn't seem planned so much as grown, something natural, inevitable, efficient, and effortless. All its paradoxes are innate."
—JIM LEWIS, *Slate*

"A simplicity and profundity worthy of Greek tragedy… *Wuthering Heights* located in Mexico and written by Kafka."
—*The Guardian*

"As a masterclass in the short story, *The Burning Plain* is a joy, but it is also a vivid historical document of a terrible and remote historical era."
—ANDY THATCHER, *The Short Review*

"There are some writers who have helped greatly to reveal the hidden identity of their people…[t]his is the case with the great Mexican writer Juan Rulfo, in my opinion the best Latin American writer of the twentieth century. He was someone who was capable of unmasking reality, in the deepest sense."
—EDUARDO GALEANO, author of *Open Veins of Latin America*

"Juan Rulfo is a master."
—PEDRO JUAN GUTIÉRREZ, author of *Tropical Animal*

"The feeling that one gets while reading [*The Burning Plain*] is of a smoky, dark night filled with suspicious shadows hiding still darker secrets that pour out of the words and sentences of the stories."
—BHUPINDER SINGH, *A Reader's Words*

THE
GOLDEN
COCKEREL
& Other Writings

—

Juan Rulfo

TRANSLATED FROM THE SPANISH
WITH AN INTRODUCTION
AND ADDITIONAL MATERIALS BY
DOUGLAS J. WEATHERFORD

DEEP VELLUM PUBLISHING

DALLAS, TEXAS

Deep Vellum Publishing
3000 Commerce St., Dallas, Texas 75226
deepvellum.org · @deepvellum

Deep Vellum Publishing is a 501c3
nonprofit literary arts organization founded in 2013.

Published by agreement with Agencia Literaria Carmen Balcells, S.A., Barcelona
El Gallo de Oro © 1980 Juan Rulfo and Heirs of Juan Rulfo
"The Secret Formula" © 2010 RM and Fundación Juan Rulfo, Mexico City
"A Letter to Clara" © 2000 Areté, Mexico City
"Life Doesn't Take Itself Very Seriously" © 1988 Era, Mexico City
"A Piece of the Night" © 1988 Era, Mexico City
"After Death," "My Aunt Cecilia," "Cleotide," "My Father," "Same as Yesterday,"
"Ángel Villalpando Was Drunk," "He Was on the Run and Hurting," "The Discoverer,"
"Ángel Pinzón Paused" © 1994 Era, Mexico City
"Castillo de Teayo" © 2002 RM, Mexico City
English translation copyright © 2017 by Douglas J. Weatherford
First edition, 2017.
All rights reserved.

ISBN: 978-1-941920-58-9 (paperback)
LIBRARY OF CONGRESS CONTROL NUMBER: 2016959432
—

The Golden Cockerel & Other Writings is published with the support of
Brigham Young University College of Humanities.
—

Cover design & typesetting by Anna Zylicz · annazylicz.com

Text set in Bembo, a typeface modeled on typefaces cut by Francesco Griffo
for Aldo Manuzio's printing of *De Aetna* in 1495 in Venice.

Distributed by Consortium Book Sales & Distribution · (800) 283-3572 · cbsd.com

Printed in the United States of America on acid-free paper.

INTRODUCTION TO
The Golden Cockerel and Other Writings

Juan Rulfo, according to one of the most persistent myths in the Latin American literary tradition, wrote only two books of fiction: a collection of short stories titled *The Plain in Flames* (*El Llano en llamas*, 1953) and a novel, *Pedro Páramo* (*Pedro Páramo*, 1955), whose title refers to the work's overbearing male protagonist. This is the literary biography of Rulfo that I learned as an undergraduate major of Spanish in the mid-1980s and it is a fabrication that continues to be told about one of the most significant writers of the twentieth century. The assertion diminishes the valuable contributions that Rulfo made as a semi-professional photographer and as a writer in the Mexican film industry. More importantly, it ignores the existence of a short novel—*The Golden Cockerel* (*El gallo de oro*, c. 1956)—that routinely and unjustly has been marginalized from the Mexican author's literary canon.[1] Indeed, the exclusion

---

1   A number of Rulfo investigators have suggested that a primary cause of the novel's marginalization was its misidentification as a film text when in 1980—nearly a quarter century after it was written and sixteen years after having first been adapted to the big screen—it was released as *The Golden Cockerel and Other Texts for the Cinema* (*El gallo de oro y otros textos para cine*). The repercussions of that label have endured and it is still possible to hear the novel incorrectly referred to as a screenplay. Despite the need to defend the generic identity of *The Golden Cockerel*, I have argued elsewhere that such advocacy should not ignore the cinematic origins of the novel that Rulfo wrote with adaptation in mind and in a period in which he was actively considering the creative and economic opportunities that writing for film might offer (see Douglas J. Weatherford, "'Texto para cine': *El gallo de oro* en la producción artística de Juan Rulfo." In *El gallo de oro* by Juan Rulfo. Mexico City: Editorial RM and Fundación Juan Rulfo, 2010. 41–73).

of *The Golden Cockerel* has been so complete that, until now, no full translation has appeared in English. *The Golden Cockerel and Other Writings* happily fills this void. The "other writings" that accompany Rulfo's second novel in the present anthology include a diverse and significant gathering of additional items penned by the author, but never included in *The Plain in Flames*. As such, *The Golden Cockerel and Other Writings* offers English-speaking readers a unique opportunity to look beyond Rulfo's most famous volumes and reconsider the creative legacy of one of Mexico's most beloved and influential writers.

JUAN RULFO: A BRIEF BIOGRAPHY

Juan Rulfo was born in 1917 in southern Jalisco, a region acutely affected by the brutality of the Mexican Revolution (1910–1917) and the Cristero Revolt (1926–1928). This turbulent period gave birth to modern Mexico and continues to shape that nation's contemporary politics, culture, and literature. Rulfo's early years were influenced by this period of violence, culminating in 1923 when his father was killed in a dispute whose origins remain vague to this day. Rulfo was six years old. His mother never recovered from the loss and died in 1927 at 32 years of age. As an orphan, Rulfo would live in a boarding school in Guadalajara, the capital of the state of Jalisco, until late adolescence when he moved to Mexico City. Although he would move between these two large cities before settling in the nation's capital, Rulfo remained deeply attracted to the small towns and countryside of rural Mexico in general and of his home state in particular.

By the early 1950s, Rulfo had abandoned his hopes of obtaining a university education (hindered in part by frequent student strikes), had worked for the government as an immigration official, and had endured an unpleasant period working for the Goodrich-Euzkadi tire company, first as a foreman and later as a traveling representative. Rulfo quit his job when he received a grant from the Mexican Writers' Center (Centro Mexicano de Escritores) and published a collection of short fiction, *The Plain in Flames* (*El Llano en llamas*). A second grant funded his first novel, *Pedro Páramo*. This innovative work challenged traditional narrative forms and helped usher in the so-called "Boom" of Latin American literature that would include such renowned writers as Carlos Fuentes (Mexico), Julio Cortázar (Argentina), and Nobel laureates Gabriel García Márquez (Colombia) and Mario Vargas Llosa (Peru). Rulfo burst onto the literary scene and, despite a relatively small corpus of published texts, the Jalisco native captured the imagination of readers around the world. To be sure, García Márquez never wavered in his praise of Rulfo's first novel, declaring that it was upon reading *Pedro Páramo* in the mid-1960s that he finally felt prepared to write *One Hundred Years of Solitude* (*Cien años de soledad*, 1967), a novel that many consider Latin America's most significant literary creation. The more than half-century that has passed since the publication of Rulfo's fiction has not diminished the author's appeal. Indeed, recent surveys of readers, writers, and academics suggest that he remains one of Mexico's most read authors at home and abroad, as new translations of his work continue to appear around the globe.

In 1962, Rulfo took an editing position at Mexico's important National Indigenist Institute (Instituto Nacional Indigenista) and remained with that organization for the remainder of his life. Although he would continue to be creative—including a limited foray writing for film—, the reserved and self-critical Rulfo mostly ignored his readers' pleas for further volumes. The most important deviation from this trend was *The Golden Cockerel*, a novel that the writer penned between 1956 and 1957 and published (perhaps reluctantly) in 1980. That same year, Rulfo released a collection of photographs (*Juan Rulfo: Homenaje nacional*) that revealed another aspect of his creative endeavors. Although he would mostly stop taking photographs by the early 1960s, the author had practiced the art form seriously during the 1940s and 1950s and exhibited his work for the first time in a small showing in Guadalajara in 1960. Recent publications have made many of Rulfo's images available, enhancing the author's reputation as one of his nation's premier photographers.

Rulfo received Mexico's National Prize for Literature (Premio Nacional de Literatura) in 1970, was elected to the Mexican Academy of Language (Academia Mexicana de la Lengua) in 1980, and received the Prince of Asturias Literary Prize in Spain in 1983. Rulfo married Clara Aparicio Reyes in 1948 and the couple had four children: Claudia, Juan Francisco, Juan Pablo, and Juan Carlos. The two youngest siblings have continued their father's creative legacy: Juan Pablo as a renowned artist and Juan Carlos as one of Mexico's most decorated documentary filmmakers. Rulfo suffered from lung cancer in his final months and died on January 7, 1986 at his home in Mexico City.

THE GOLDEN COCKEREL: THE HISTORICAL, CULTURAL, AND GEOGRAPHICAL BACKGROUND

In the fall of 1910, Mexico was a country on the verge of revolution. Porfirio Díaz occupied the presidency and, through corruption and coercion, had managed to stay in office since 1876. Although the dictator oversaw significant efforts to modernize Mexico's economy and infrastructure, those endeavors failed to alleviate the suffering and discontent of the nation's majority poor. In November of 1910, after Díaz fraudulently claimed victory in the most recent elections and prepared to begin his eighth term in office, a number of factions declared open rebellion. The armed intervention that followed would be known as the Mexican Revolution and gave the nation a new pantheon of heroes, including Emiliano Zapata and Francisco "Pancho" Villa. Although Díaz would flee the country in May of 1911, fighting would continue for many years as various insurgent leaders sought control of the country. By 1917, Venustiano Carranza had consolidated power in the capital and a new constitution was drafted. The consequences of the Revolution had been profound: more than a million Mexican soldiers, insurgents, and civilians perished, the countryside was devastated, and many cities and towns were left in ruins. Although many historians consider the adoption of the 1917 Constitution as the official end of the Revolution, violence would persist for years to come, culminating in a second armed insurrection, the Cristero Revolt (1926-1928), which was particularly fierce in Rulfo's home state of Jalisco.

Mexico struggled to define the meaning of the Revolution in the years following that upheaval. Although early political leaders extolled the ideals of the movement, they were all too eager to return to Porfirio Díaz's penchant for the façade of democracy. Power was eventually consolidated in a dominant political organization, the Institutional Revolutionary Party (Partido Revolucionario Institucional, or PRI), which would rule the nation with only limited opposition for the next seven decades, until Vicente Fox of the National Action Party (Partido Acción Nacional, or PAN) assumed the presidency in 2000. In its rhetoric, the PRI promoted itself as the political heir to the ideals of the Revolution and yet worked only sporadically to implement those principles. For example, although one of the most visible objectives of the 1910 uprising (especially for the followers of Villa and Zapata) was agrarian reform, the issue was not taken up passionately until the presidency of Lázaro Cárdenas from 1934–1940, and then quietly diminished during later administrations.

In the decades following the Revolution, Mexico's artists and intellectuals differed in their evaluation of their nation's condition. The ruling party saw the value of rallying the country around a mostly upbeat and idealistic view of the insurgent past and provided significant funding to writers, filmmakers, and artists through various government agencies. Most Mexicans felt a genuine sympathy for the suffering of the impoverished and were eager to embrace the ideals of the Revolution as a national myth. Diego Rivera and his fellow muralists, for example, were frequent recipients of government-backed funding and their larger-than-life paintings often extolled the virtues of this new national creed. Although there are advantages to the model of cooperation between government and artist that Mexico developed in the post-Revolution decades, it is also true that this interdependence helped soften criticism of a society that had clearly failed to adequately improve many of the inequalities that gave birth to the 1910 uprising. Not all artists were willing to restrain their criticism, however, and their work reflects a growing sense, especially in the 1940s and 1950s, that the nation faced major problems.[2] With the publication of *The Plain in Flames* and *Pedro Páramo*, Juan Rulfo rejected the tendency of so many mid-century Mexican politicians and artists to remember the past nostalgically and he emerged as one of the most discerning observers of life in the Mexican countryside during the first half of the twentieth century. In that sense, *The Golden Cockerel* fits perfectly within Rulfo's canon as an honest reading of the Mexican condition. That is not to suggest that this short novel is an overtly political treatise. Indeed, Rulfo avoids references that would place the action of his story in a specific moment in time. The novel never indicates the year and there are no direct references to the Revolution, to the Cristero Revolt, to efforts at agrarian reform, or to any other historical event. Moreover, the author never reveals whether his characters travel from town to town by foot, animal, train, or automobile. This lack of specificity lends a timeless quality to the story and allows the reader to place the action in various moments of Mexican history.

---

2   One might consider, for example, the photojournalism of Nacho López who documented many of the social ills of Mexico City or the withering film *The Young and the Damned* (*Los olvidados*, 1950) by Spanish director Luis Buñuel who had found refuge from European conflicts in Mexico. Meanwhile, the novel *The Book of Lamentations* (*Oficio de tinieblas*, 1962) by Rosario Castellanos stands out as one literary example of a scathing examination of Mexico's failure to live up to its revolutionary ideals.

Nonetheless, there is good reason to imagine *The Golden Cockerel* as taking place in the years following the Revolution, perhaps during the mid-1950s in which it was written. The lack of any mention of armed intervention reasonably rules out the 1910s and 1920s as the novel's setting, while the author's preference for placing his fiction in the twentieth century makes the ensuing decades the work's likely timeframe.[3] Indeed, the depressed economic opportunities of rural Mexico depicted in the novel can be seen as a reflection of the post-Revolution period. Placed in such a chronological setting, *The Golden Cockerel* continues Rulfo's impulse to expose the failure of the Revolution to affect real change for Mexico's impoverished, a sensibility that he developed so well in *Pedro Páramo* and in many of the stories collected in *The Plain in Flames* (see, among others, "It's Because We're So Poor," "Paso del Norte," and "They Have Given Us the Land").

Although Rulfo preferred to mask the precise chronological moment of his novel, he was more concrete when it came to placing his characters in their geographical environment. Indeed, Dionisio Pinzón and Bernarda Cutiño (also known as *La Caponera*) show up at a variety of communities both large (e.g. Aguascalientes and Zacatecas) and small (e.g. San Miguel del Milagro and Árbol Grande) that dot Mexico's provincial landscape. Despite this geographical diversity, the action of the novel takes place

---

3　Two film adaptations of the novel are more concrete in their choice of a chronological setting. *The Golden Cockerel* (*El gallo de oro*; dir. Roberto Gavaldón, 1964) shows automobiles used alongside horses and buggies in what might be the early 1930s. *The Reign of Fortune* (*El imperio de la fortuna*; dir. Arturo Ripstein, 1985) places the action in a more contemporary moment, perhaps the mid-1980s in which it was filmed.

predominantly in or near the important agricultural region of central Mexico, known as the Bajío, that includes portions of the states of Guanajuato, Querétaro, Aguascalientes, and Jalisco, an area to the north of Mexico's capital that Rulfo knew well.[4] And yet, as is so common in the author's literary canon, the geography of *The Golden Cockerel* is not limited to the real; rather it is part of the novel's figurative structure. It is significant, for example, that Rulfo never mentions Mexico City or Guadalajara, perhaps hinting at the inability of central governments (national or state) to positively impact the lives of everyday Mexicans. Other gaps in the novel's descriptions of place are significant. For example, Rulfo seldom describes unique features that would distinguish one settlement from another, preferring instead to place his characters in locales that are notable for their similarity from one town to another: cantinas, gambling halls, and cockfighting rings. This spatial monotony suggests the boredom that can plague the experience of those, like Dionisio and Bernarda (and Juan Rulfo who had worked previously as a traveling salesman for a tire company), who make their living on the road. Ironically, it also calls into question the freedom that *La Caponera* claims for herself as a wandering singer of songs. Despite her ambulatory lifestyle, Bernarda inhabits the same spaces, suggesting, perhaps, that her real entrapment began long before Dionisio forced her to remain by his side in the overwhelming solitude of their estate at Santa Gertrudis.

---

4   Many of the towns mentioned in *The Golden Cockerel* appear as well in one of Mexico's most important novels of the Revolution, *The Underdogs* (*Los de abajo*, 1915) by Mariano Azuela: Aguascalientes, Celaya, Cuquío, among others. This connection might be seen as another attempt by the author to connect his novel to the context of the Mexican Revolution.

Notwithstanding the sense of enclosure (spatial, but also social and economic) that follows and eventually overwhelms his characters, wandering remains a significant element of Rulfo's novel. Indeed, one might see in Dionisio and Bernarda's constant travels the devotion of those who seek transcendence through pilgrimage. This figurative potential of the novel's environment is immediately clear in the hometown that Rulfo chose for his protagonist. Dionisio hails from San Miguel del Milagro, or Saint Michael of the Miracle. The religious connotations of the name likely appealed to Rulfo who was frequently interested in the metaphoric qualities of place names.[5] The actual town of San Miguel del Milagro is located in the state of Tlaxcala, near the archeological site of Cacaxtla. Despite its small size (currently just over 1,100 inhabitants), the town has been, and remains, an important pilgrimage site for many faithful Catholics who believe that Saint Michael appeared there in 1631. And yet, Rulfo's allusions to devotion are not limited to the figurative, nor are they free of censure. Instead, both the presence and the absence of the religious are steeped in *The Golden Cockerel*'s realism and in its disparaging view of Mexican society. What the novel does not show is perhaps as important as what it does. For example, although Dionisio does "commend himself to the Lord" before pitting his cockerel, none of the characters of the novel are seen attending mass or visiting the confessional, suggesting that the church is not a vital force in one's daily life. And when the church does appear, what the novel highlights is that

---

5   The best examples are found in *Pedro Páramo*, where the cursed town of Comala, for example, alludes to the heat associated with a "comal," a traditional Mexican griddle used to warm tortillas.

institution's failings as a mediator of both the temporal and eternal well-being of its congregants. As the novel opens, for example, an impoverished and malnourished Dionisio goes in search of a wayward cow whose owner, the local priest, will pay for this service only with the abstract and insincere promise of some future blessing in Heaven. The detachment of the church in *The Golden Cockerel* is ironic since many of the festivals and fairs that attract Dionisio and Bernarda are based on local religious celebrations. In the novel's action, however, the chapel and faithful devotion are barely visible while secular and irreverent festivities—dominated by gambling and song—spring up on the church's periphery while taking center stage.

Rulfo's commentary on the church extends to the government and to an economy that seems to entrap rather than liberate. Again, however, Rulfo is circuitous in his censure and government officials appear in the novel only twice.[6] Dionisio contends with his hometown mayor who will not permit him to disinter his mother's remains, and he later encounters a couple of blustering and narcissistic politicians at one of his cockfights. Rulfo's most profound commentary on the Mexican condition at mid-century, nonetheless, might be found in what is missing from his novel: opportunity. As *The Golden Cockerel* opens, Dionisio and his mother are described as being on the verge of starvation. A

---

6   Rulfo is not always so indirect in his representation of church and state. "They Have Given Us the Land" ("Nos han dado la tierra"), for example, is a scathing indictment of the void that exists between the political rhetoric of agrarian reform and that movement's actual results. Meanwhile, the inhabitants of *Pedro Páramo*, languishing in a purgatory between Heaven and Hell, are constantly connected to a sense of the religious and to Father Rentería, the official arbiter of the Catholic Church in the town of Comala.

disfigured arm makes it impossible for Rulfo's protagonist to work "as a laborer or as a farmhand, the only occupations that were to be had in town," and he survives on what little he is able to earn as a town crier. Although he is described as "one of the poorest men of San Miguel del Milagro," Dionisio should not be seen as unique. Rather, he is emblematic of the economic struggles of so many rural Mexicans. The pessimism of such a message becomes only more acute if we imagine that Rulfo has placed the action of his novel in the decades following a revolution that, despite government propaganda, has failed to improve the lives of the most vulnerable. And yet Rulfo's tale is one that involves extreme economic mobility as Dionisio Pinzón, in the company of Bernarda who serves as a good-luck charm, becomes wealthy through cockfighting and games of chance. Nonetheless, *The Golden Cockerel* does not advocate for Dionisio's path to prosperity. To be sure, in an earlier version of the text, Rulfo considered a title, *From Nothing to Nothing* (*De la nada a la nada*), that hints at his protagonist's ultimate demise. It might also be seen as a commentary on an economic system where hard work is insufficient to achieve a dignified life. Rulfo does not condemn Dionisio's desire for a better future, but since his protagonist becomes bitter and despotic as his wealth increases, the author does imply that his is not a path that will improve the fortunes of the individual or of the nation.

Even so, Rulfo's novel is not a facile denunciation where judgment is easily rendered. Indeed, *The Golden Cockerel* is, in many ways, a celebration of Mexico's ability to embrace life despite hardship, a stubborn optimism seen especially in the music that Bernarda and her mariachi band perform night after night.

Through it all, the novel embraces an ambivalence that neither sanctifies nor demonizes its protagonists. Dionisio is a down-on-his-luck underdog who demands our sympathy before descending into narcissism and becoming his wife's captor. Bernarda is a headstrong woman whose struggle for self-reliance is repeatedly compromised by the dubious alliances she is willing to accept with men. Dionisio and Bernarda are both real and archetypal and together they belong in the pantheon of Rulfo's most memorable characters and might be read as variations on Pedro Páramo and Susana San Juan, the hauntingly iconic protagonists of the author's first novel.

Rulfo's unwillingness to offer easy condemnation can be found as well in his representation of games of chance. In the half century since the author wrote *The Golden Cockerel*, cockfighting has been discredited and many nations have outlawed the practice. Although cocking remains popular in a number of countries with longstanding cultural ties to the sport (among them Mexico, the Dominican Republic, Colombia, and the Philippines), increased public aversion to the activity is likely to lead to bans even in these locations. Cockfighting is clearly significant in the novel and the author borrows his title from the small but intrepid rooster that will change Dionisio's destiny. Moreover, Rulfo describes the golden cockerel's battles with sufficient detail to suggest that he was at least somewhat familiar with the sport. Yet it would be inaccurate to see the title as a nod to the centrality of cockfighting in the novel or as an approbation of that endeavor.[7]

---

7   Roberto Gavaldón retained the original title of Rulfo's novel when he directed the first adaptation of the novel in 1964 (*El gallo de oro*). Arturo Ripstein,

To be sure, Dionisio's gold-colored bird dies before the novel's halfway mark and the town-crier-turned-cockfighter quickly moves on to various games of chance. The prominence of the cockerel in the work's label might better be understood as the author's desire to universalize his rags-to-riches-to-rags story. A golden cockerel (or *gallo de oro*) is a fairly recognizable token of good fortune, for example, and can be found to this day as the name of numerous restaurants and bars across Latin America (and in Hispanic neighborhoods of the United States). Nonetheless, Rulfo's novel is not a celebration of gambling, nor is it an endorsement of cockfighting. Although the Jalisco native seldom judges in his narratives and presents his characters—sinners all—without heavy-handed moralizing, he does offer a commentary against the brutality of a blood sport that, according to the third-person narrator, contributes to the protagonist's debasement:

> It didn't take long for Dionisio to stop being that humble man that we had known in San Miguel del Milagro, who, having at first only one bird as his entire fortune, always appeared restless and nervous and, scared of losing, always commended himself to the Lord before competing. Yet little by little his very nature was becoming something else through his exposure to the violent sport of cockfighting,

---

on the other hand, chose to minimize the importance of the cockerel in his later adaptation that he titled *The Empire of Fortune* (*El imperio de la fortuna*, 1985). As a translator, I also vacillated with the title and considered using *The Fortunes of Dionisio Pinzón*, an alteration that would recognize Ripstein's variation and one that might better suggest the broader themes of destiny and chance that the novel develops. Ultimately, I felt that it was more appropriate to conserve Rulfo's original title.

as if the thick, reddish liquid coming from those dying animals had turned him to stone, transforming him into a cold and calculating man, sure and confident in the path of his destiny. (75)

As such, Rulfo's novel is not a simplistic tale. It revels in the world of fairs and festivals that dot the Bajío region of Mexico without succumbing to a folkloric veneration of that domain.

In many ways, *The Golden Cockerel* is unique in Rulfo's literary canon. It is less polished and more oral than his previous writings. It has few chronological breaks, longer sentences, and is less experimental than his other two publications. Nonetheless, this second novel fits nicely into Rulfo's creative canon. It returns to the small-town geography of central Mexico where his characters, despite the ideals of the Mexican Revolution, endure in a world still marked by the weight of poverty and injustice. More than sixty years after the novel's composition, *The Golden Cockerel* deserves to find a wider audience and to finally take its place alongside *The Plain in Flames* and *Pedro Páramo* and put to rest the misguided proclamation that Juan Rulfo was the author of only two books of fiction.

BEYOND THE PLAIN IN FLAMES:

AN INTRODUCTION TO JUAN RULFO'S "OTHER WRITINGS"

The "other writings" of the present anthology are an eclectic mix of short items that offer an intriguing look into the Jalisco native's creative production beyond the stories canonized in *The Plain in Flames*. All texts were chosen in close consultation with Víctor Jiménez, director of the Fundación Juan Rulfo, and members of the Rulfo family. To be sure, as the selection process advanced, it became clear that the collection that we were putting together for English translation deserved an audience in Spanish as well, resulting in the early 2017 release of *El gallo de oro y otros relatos* published by the Fundación Juan Rulfo and Editorial RM.

The three best-known of these "other writings"—one with a poetic structure that was written for film ("The Secret Formula") and two narrative pieces ("Life Doesn't Take Itself Very Seriously" and "A Piece of the Night")—were published during Rulfo's lifetime but never included in *The Plain in Flames*. Although each of these has appeared previously in English translation,[8] their frequent isolation within Rulfo's *oeuvre* makes them perfect additions to this collection dedicated to making a wider selection of one of Latin America's most significant writers available to an English-speaking audience. Two additional items—one letter and the fictionalized travel narrative "Castillo de Teayo"—have already earned a place in Rulfo's canon through posthumous publications.[9]

---

8   Deborah Owen Moore, for example, translated these texts (along with "The Spoils") and published them in *TriQuarterly* (#100, Fall 1997, pp. 164-80).

9   The letters that Rulfo wrote from 1944 to 1950 to his fiancée/wife, were collected in 2000 in *Aire de las colinas: Cartas a Clara* (Mexico City: Areté). "Castillo de Teayo" has appeared recently in multiple locations, including *Juan Rulfo:*

The remaining items—nine narrative fragments—are less definitive in their generic and canonic identity and have been published almost exclusively in *Juan Rulfo's Notebooks* [*Los cuadernos de Juan Rulfo*].[10]

"THE SECRET FORMULA" ["La fórmula secreta"] is unique among Juan Rulfo's writings for its poetic structure. Although it is possible that someone other than the author gave the text the form with which it is associated, there is no mistaking that Rulfo, a master of the narrative form, imagined this piece as a lyrical response to the marginalization and suffering of Mexico's poor. Rulfo wrote "The Secret Formula" at the invitation of Rubén Gámez who used the text as a voiceover narration to accompany portions of his experimental film by the same title (*La fórmula secreta*, 1964), an allusion to the ingredients of Coca Cola and a critique, among other things, of the influence of the United States on Mexico. The well-known and highly regarded narrative was paired with another short filmic piece, "The Spoils" ["El despojo"] and published in 1980 alongside Rulfo's second novel in *The Golden Cockerel and Other Texts for the Cinema* [*El gallo de oro y otros textos para cine*]. "The Spoils" is difficult to appreciate when unaccompanied by the film to which it belongs (*El despojo*, 1960, dir. Antonio Reynoso) and, for that reason, was not included in the present anthology.

"LIFE DOESN'T TAKE ITSELF VERY SERIOUSLY" ["La vida no es

Letras e imágenes (Mexico City: Editorial RM, 2002, pp. 47–55, with an English translation by Gregory Dechant on pp. 188–90).

10   Juan Rulfo, *Los cuadernos de Juan Rulfo*. Pres. Clara Aparicio de Rulfo. Transcription Yvette Jiménez de Báez. Mexico City: Era, 1994. At least three of these items appeared in Mexico City newspapers after the author's death ("Iba adolorido. Amodorrado de cansancio," "Después de la muerte," and "Mi padre").

muy seria en sus cosas"] was released originally in the Mexican journal *América* on June 30, 1945 (#40, pp. 35–36) and, as such, is the author's earliest published piece. Although it appeared in other locations during Rulfo's life and after his passing, the author chose not to include this story in *The Plain in Flames*. The title ("La vida no es muy seria en sus cosas") presents some immediate problems for the translator and I considered a number of options, including "Life Is Not to Be Taken So Seriously" and "Life Has a Way of Playing Tricks on You." The lighthearted potential of Rulfo's original needs to be tempered by the somber foreshadowing of the story's events and, in the end, I chose to retain the title of the English translation of the story published by Deborah Owen Moore in *TriQuarterly* (Fall 1997, #100, pp. 177–179).

"A PIECE OF THE NIGHT" ["Un pedazo de noche"] also enjoyed fairly wide distribution during Rulfo's life. Although it was first published in September of 1959 in the journal *Revista Mexicana de Literatura* (Nueva Época #3, pp. 7–14), an annotation at the bottom of the page listed its date of composition as January 1940. The story is, in reality, a fragment of an urban novel, tentatively titled *El hijo del desaliento*, that the author was composing before deciding to abandon the project. Despite its uncommon urban setting, "A Piece of the Night" is very Rulfian in nature with an encounter between a prostitute and a gravedigger, two life-weary protagonists whose nocturnal wanderings in search of shelter and with an infant in tow connect them archetypally and ironically to the Holy Family.

"A LETTER TO CLARA" was written at the end of February of

1947. At the time, Rulfo was living in Mexico City and working as a foreman at the Goodrich-Euzkadi tire company. Although the position, obtained with the help of relatives, represented an important opportunity, Rulfo despised the work. In this letter, the young author combines playful banter with his fiancée with existential observations about the dehumanizing nature of the factory work that he and his workers endured on a daily basis (he would later transfer to a preferable position as a traveling salesman). In this very personal letter, Clara Aparicio Reyes, who remained at home in Guadalajara, is Rulfo's clear source of hope for the future and he calls her by a couple of diminutive pet names: Mayecita and Chachinita. The couple would marry in August of 1948.

"CASTILLO DE TEAYO" is a travel narrative that often feels like a short story. Its description of an archaeological zone reflects Rulfo's life-long passion for Mexican history, especially its pre-Colombian roots. The typewritten original of this text includes the signature of Juan de la Cosa, a pseudonym that the author used from time to time and that refers to an early Spanish explorer and cartographer. Rulfo published a number of photographs of Castillo de Teayo, Veracruz in the January 1952 edition of *Mapa*, a travel journal sponsored by the Goodrich-Euzkadi tire company. Rulfo was in charge of this particular edition of *Mapa* and it is likely that he wrote "Castillo de Teayo" with the idea that it would accompany his photographs. If that is the case, it is unclear why it was ultimately left out. A selection of Rulfo's photographs of the Castillo de Teayo archeological site is included following this narrative piece. *Juan Rulfo's Notebooks* [*Los cuadernos de Juan Rulfo*] is a unique gathering of Rulfo's unpublished—and, in many cases, unfinished— writings. Authorized by the author's widow, the collection appeared in 1994, giving readers a glimpse into Rulfo's creative process. The texts of *Juan Rulfo's Notebooks* are eclectic in nature and include early drafts of *Pedro Páramo*, fragments of a film script, portions of two novels that the author began and never completed, and other experimental writings. The nine items from this collection that were identified for inclusion in the present anthology are unique creative explorations that fit well into Rulfo's literary *oeuvre* and exhibit clear narrative structures that allow them to be read as independent story-like texts.

"AFTER DEATH," "MY AUNT CECILIA," and "CLEOTILDE" were included in a section of *Juan Rulfo's Notebooks* titled "On the Road to the Novel" ("Camino a la novela") to indicate their independence as literary texts while still seeming to be variations—writing exercises if you will— on the people, places, and themes that would eventually lead Rulfo to write *Pedro Páramo*. Other items included in *Los cuadernos de Juan Rulfo* are clearly drafts of Rulfo's best known novel and are collected under the heading: "Fragments of *Pedro Páramo*" ["Fragmentos de *Pedro Páramo*"]. Three of these items are of particular interest and are included here. "MY FATHER" ["Mi padre"] is a highly personal text in which a first-person narrator tries to understand the violent demise of his father. Although the piece might be read as belonging to the voice of a young and still innocent Pedro Páramo, the reader who recalls the death of Rulfo's own father to an assassin's bullet might discern a suffering that is more real than invented. "SAME AS YESTERDAY" ["Igual que ayer, dijo el padre"] explores the struggles of a local priest to resist temptation in the form of the intriguing and beautiful Susana San Juan. Although appearing in this fragment as Father Villalpando, this aroused cleric is none other than Father Rentería from Rulfo's first novel, tasked with giving the last rites to the second wife of Pedro Páramo, a woman who is lost to insanity in erotic memories of a previous husband.

This introspective protagonist appears as well in the fragment titled "SUSANA FOSTER," where a distinctive surname, like that of Villalpando in the previous story, offers an example of how Rulfo often tried out different labels for his characters and his places in early drafts of his writings.[11] In early drafts of his seminal novel, for example, even Pedro Páramo is first known as Maurilio Gutiérrez.

Two items included in this anthology were compiled in *The Notebooks of Juan Rulfo* under the heading "Story Manuscripts" ["Manuscritos de relatos"]. The first, "HE WAS ON THE RUN AND HURTING" ["Iba adolorido," sometimes referred to as "Los girasoles" or "The Sunflowers"], is an exploration of the passage of time in the moment of death and recalls American author Ambrose Bierce's famous "An Occurrence at Owl Creek Bridge" whose structure was later re-imagined by the Argentine writer Jorge Luis Borges as "The Secret Miracle" ("El milagro secreto"). "ÁNGEL PINZÓN PAUSED" ["Ángel Pinzón se detuvo"] is part of a section labeled "Manuscripts Attributable to *La cordillera*" ["Manuscritos atribuibles a *La cordillera*"]. *La cordillera* (or *The Mountain*

---

11   I have suggested elsewhere that Rulfo's choice of "Foster" for his female protagonist could be a nod to his interest in Orson Welles's iconic Charles Foster Kane. See "*Citizen Kane* y *Pedro Páramo*: Un análisis comparativo." Coord. Víctor Jiménez, Alberto Vital, and Jorge Zepeda. *Tríptico para Juan Rulfo: Poesía, fotografía, crítica*. Mexico City: Fundación Juan Rulfo-Editorial RM, 2006, pp. 501–30.

Range), a novel that Rulfo worked on without ever completing, was a frequent subject in the interviews that he gave after 1955 as reporters and investigators hoped to learn when the influential author would publish again. Finally, "THE DISCOVERER" ["El descubridor"], the second piece of this anthology that appeared in *Juan Rulfo's Notebooks* as a "Story Manuscript," is a fascinating look at race identity in Mexico. The tale, as one critic has suggested, was likely written in response to the massacre of student protesters in Mexico City's Plaza de Tlatelolco in 1968,[12] making it, chronologically, the most recent piece included in the present anthology and the obvious one to bring it to a close.

Juan Rulfo's Notebooks was controversial when it appeared in 1994. Clara Aparicio de Rulfo, the author's widow, began a note to the readers of this collection of unpublished writings with an ominous tone: "It would seem that what I am doing is a terrible thing. That's what some of the individuals with whom I have consulted about publishing the texts from Juan's working notebooks have made me feel. I've thought that it's possible."[13] *Juan Rulfo's Notebooks*, as the author's widow understood, might be seen as an invasion into the creative world of a beloved writer. Nonetheless, Doña Clara resisted the temptation to conceal these texts that her husband had so carefully crafted, but without deciding to send them to press. Her response to her detractors is a tender one. She understands the danger of her decision while feeling the need, ultimately, to share the literary treasure that her husband left to

---

12   See Alberto Vital, *Noticias sobre Juan Rulfo: 1784–2003*. Mexico City: Editorial RM, 2004, p. 179.

13   "A los lectores." In Juan Rulfo, *Los cuadernos de Juan Rulfo*, p. 7; translation mine.

her: "But something happens inside of me every time I look over the pages of these notebooks: each word, each phrase, full of life experiences and feelings, make me reflect on the need to share these tales that are so full of him...."[14] It is possible, of course, that some, like those who questioned the release of *Juan Rulfo's Notebooks*, will wonder about the present anthology, an edition that looks to extend Rulfo's literary legacy beyond the two books that gained him such a prestigious reputation. To those individuals, I hope to respond with the same kindhearted understanding of Doña Clara. It is my belief that *The Golden Cockerel and Other Writings* is a unique and valuable collection that bears witness to Juan Rulfo and deserves to exist because each text is "so full of him."

---

14   Ibid.

TRANSLATOR'S NOTE

In a particular scene of Juan Rulfo's first novel, *Pedro Páramo*, the local priest, Father Rentería, is overwhelmed by a chorus of women's voices whose persistent and repeated confessions of the sins they have committed seem to echo in the tormented cleric's mind and soul. That image comes eerily to mind as I begin to write this translator's note, an exercise not uncommon among those who dare to reconstruct an author's original tale in a different language. Translation is not a facile and trouble-free activity. Even the most congenial approach requires the translator to commit some level of violence to the previous text in an effort to fashion a work that will connect with a new audience that reads with different linguistic and cultural eyes. Thus, with metaphorical blood on his or her hands, the translator writes a "note," confessing to sins—both of commission and omission—committed during the act of rendition, hoping that an honest explanation of difficult decisions made will satisfy the demands of justice and result in a more generous reading. I assume that all translators, as my analogy suggests, feel some sense of remorse for alterations they make. And yet such a perspective is one-sided: it ignores the adoration for another's work that is at the heart of the act of adaptation. In such a light, translation is an optimistic and joyful activity that values communication across linguistic, temporal, cultural, and national boundaries. I have translated *The Golden Cockerel* (*El gallo de oro*, c. 1956) and a selection of other writings because I value the artistic world of Juan Rulfo, and I believe that these texts demand to be read by a wider audience.[15] I am thrilled to offer this translation, and I hope, consequently, that my "translator's note" will feel less like the confession of a miscreant and more like the thoughtful reflections of a delighted devotee.

Rulfo's two seminal works, *The Plain in Flames* (*El Llano en llamas*, 1953) and *Pedro Páramo* (1955) are defined by a narrative that is often experimental and challenging, as well as abbreviated and poetic. The author's style in those two volumes is easily identifiable and highly esteemed. *The Golden Cockerel*, as I argue in my introduction, is clearly a product of Rulfo's literary, cultural, and geographic landscape, and it deserves a place among the canon of one of Mexico's greatest writers of fiction. Even so, readers of *The Plain in Flames* and *Pedro Páramo* will notice a clear stylistic difference that makes *The Golden Cockerel* a unique offering. In this second novel, Rulfo's writing is more fluid and informal and avoids the more complex narrative tendencies of his earlier

---

15   For my translation of *The Golden Cockerel* and "The Secret Formula," I used the updated and corrected versions of those texts that were published in 2010 (Juan Rulfo. *El gallo de oro*. Mexico City: Editorial RM-Fundación Juan Rulfo, 2010.). For "Life Doesn't Take Itself Very Seriously" and "A Piece of the Night" I relied upon the versions that were included in a so-called personal anthology of the author's work (Juan Rulfo. *Antología personal*. Prol. Jorge Ruffinelli. Mexico City: Era, 1988.). I used the version of "Castillo de Teayo" that is found in *Juan Rulfo: Letras e imágenes* (Mexico City: Editorial RM, 2002). "A Letter to Clara" is collected in *Aire de las Colinas: Cartas a Clara* (Mexico City: Areté, 2000). All other texts are included in Juan Rulfo, *Los cuadernos de Juan Rulfo* (Pres. Clara Aparicio de Rulfo. Transcription Yvette Jiménez de Báez. Mexico City: Era, 1994).

fiction (the switching between narrators of *Pedro Páramo*, for example). The more relaxed narrative structure of Rulfo's subsequent novel does not free the text from translation complications. In *The Golden Cockerel*, for example, Rulfo abandons the short, often staccato-like sentences and descriptions of *Pedro Páramo* and *The Plain in Flames* for long and elaborate sentences, divided by multiple commas and semi-colons, a tendency that often reflects an oral quality. For the most part, I have retained that stylistic element, as in this example where the third-person omniscient narrator describes Bernarda Cutiño:

> As far as anyone could tell, since her days as a small child *La Caponera* had roamed from town to town in the company of her mother, a poor wanderer in search of festivals, up until that moment when, with her mother dead from a fire in one of the tents, she came to rely on her own wits, joining up with one of those groups of traveling musicians who just take to the road attentive to whatever Providence might decide to send their way. (68)

There are times, however, when it felt preferable to divide Rulfo's longer sentences to avoid a style that might seem unwieldy and unnatural in contemporary English. Additionally, Rulfo often uses short paragraphs, many of which are no more than one or two sentences in length. The longer sentences and shorter paragraphs are part of the more casual—even oral—nature of *The Golden Cockerel*. Although I retained most examples of this style, there were a few moments where I preferred to combine two or more shorter paragraphs. There are other instances where I felt that a slight departure from the original would improve the readability of the novel in English without significant deviation from Rulfo's intent. Likewise, there are times (especially in the use of vocabulary) where I chose to remain completely faithful to the text when a variation might have been warranted. I hope that the following discussion of a few of the decisions that I made as a translator will prove useful.

It is well known that Rulfo was interested in the sound of his prose and, although a few of his texts reproduce the speech of his rural protagonists, the Jalisco native employed the vernacular only sparingly. That is true in *The Golden Cockerel* as well where the author uses geography and culture, more than local language, to place the action of his novel in the Bajío region of Mexico during the mid-twentieth century. To be sure, the landscape that the novel traverses and the festival life of cockfights, cantinas, and games of chance that the characters experience bring out a local atmosphere that Rulfo savors. And yet Rulfo is not interested only in the regional and his cautious use of the vernacular suggests a desire to fashion a narrative (like *Pedro Páramo*) that, beyond the native, possesses an inclusive and timeless quality. A desire to capture both the universal and the regional qualities of *The Golden Cockerel* is at the heart of my decision to retain a modest selection of words and phrases in their original Spanish. A few of those are simply left un-translated and in regular type (e.g. pesos, tequila, cerveza, amigo), an indication that these are labels that are commonly known to English speakers in the United States. Other expressions that are left untranslated are italicized to indicate their less common nature (e.g. *mezcal, político, rebozo*). These are words and phrases that have a significant cultural component, are problematic in translation, or add a local flavor, without being awkward within the English translation. Whether italicized or not, expressions left in Spanish are explained in a glossary at the end of this publication.

Among the more visible examples of uncommon terms that I left in their original are the nicknames of two of Rulfo's unforgettable characters: *La Caponera* and *Quiebranueces*. In *The Golden Cockerel*, Bernarda Cutiño is known as *La Caponera* and, although critics have debated the precise meaning and importance of this label, Alfred Mac Adam, who translated a short segment of the novel, chose to render the term into English as *Lead Mare* (referring to the horse that is placed at the front since other animals tend to follow it).[16] Mac Adam's selection is not inaccurate and certainly conveys Rulfo's idea that Bernarda is to be seen as a headstrong and domineering woman. Still, it seems unnecessarily awkward and unable to abide the wider variety of connotations that a reader might take from the original. My preference was to leave *La Caponera* alone. After all, the novelist offers his own explanation within the text of what the term might connote: "At the front of them all was a tough and attractive woman with a flashy

---

16   Mac Adam's translation (that he titled *The Golden Cock*) covered only the first few pages of Rulfo's second novel (*Review: Latin American Literature and Arts*. Vol. 26.46, 1992, pp. 37–41). Full translations of *El gallo de oro* have appeared in German (*Der goldene Hahn. Mit einem weiteren Filmtext des Autors un einem Nachwort von Jorge Ayala Blanco*. Trans. Mariana Frenk-Westeheim. Munich: Carl Hanser Verlag, 1984), French (*Le coq d'or et autres textes pour le cinéma*. Trans. Grabriel Iaculli. Paris: Gallimard, 1993), Italian (*Il gallo d'oro*. Trans. Dario Puccini. Rome: Riuniti, 1983), and Portuguese (*O galo de ouro e outros textos para cinema*. Trans. Eric Nepomuceno. Rio de Janeiro: Civilização Brasileira, 1999).

rebozo worn across her chest who they called *La Caponera*, perhaps on account of the sway she held over men" (43). Likewise, the pimp who lords over Pilar in "A Piece of the Night" and initiates her into the profession is called the *Quiebranueces*. Deborah Owen Moore, who in 1997 published an English-language version of this short narrative text in the journal *TriQuarterly*, rendered the epithet very literally as the "Nutcracker."[17] Again, I felt that the term was inopportune when imagined in English and that the sexual violence that the nickname implies was as clear, if not more so, when left in the original Spanish.

Translating the novel's very regional world of cockfighting and games of chance also proved challenging. Rulfo's detailed descriptions of gaming and gambling suggest his familiarity with these activities. The question became whether to retain the unique local elements of this domain, or alter them for easier consumption by an English-speaking audience. Although few readers will have any real experience with cockfighting, the vocabulary associated with that activity (e.g. breasting, pitting, cockpit) is unlikely to be problematic. The process of judging those matches and, especially, of betting on them will likely be more puzzling. Ultimately, it seemed preferable to preserve the authenticity (and the confusion for many readers) of these endeavors, and I offer only minimal interventions to help explain what is taking place. After all, it is the feel of this realm rather than an exact knowledge of its inner workings that Rulfo is most trying to communicate. This is true as well when it comes to the many games of chance (especially card games) that

---

17   Moore also completed translations of "The Secret Formula," "The Spoils," and "Life Doesn't Take Itself Very Seriously" (see *TriQuarterly*, #100, Fall 1997, pp. 164–80).

are described throughout the novel. Most readers will find these contests perplexing since Rulfo's characters use Spanish playing cards, with their differing suits and values, rather than the French variety most commonly seen in the English-speaking world. The unfamiliar nature of the games that are played is, nonetheless, part of the joy of reading *The Golden Cockerel* and indicate quite clearly, beyond the universality of his text, that the Jalisco native is showing us a world that is dependent on a regional reality.

There are times, nonetheless, when I do choose to deviate from Rulfo's original in an attempt to make the work more readable for an English-language audience. An example of this tendency can be found in the terms that I use to translate the word *gallo* (rooster). *Gallo* is quite important to the novel's storyline, of course, and the term appears regularly throughout the text. Notably, Rulfo offers few synonyms to *gallo* and the word's recurrence renders it distinctly redundant. The scattered use of *animal* (animal) and *animalito* (little animal) are clear exceptions, along with quite a few nounal adjectives (adjectives that function as a noun) that are found throughout: *el de Chihuahua* (the one from Chihuahua), *el cocolote* (the timid one), *el ciego* (the blind one), among others. As I began to translate Rulfo's novel, it seemed that following the author's original style and selecting only one equivalent for *gallo* would be insufficient. Although the word is common in Spanish and is the clear choice for Rulfo as he describes the male chicken, the options in translation are not as simple. In English, *gallo* can be a rooster, a cock, or a cockerel. A turn toward the more technical vocabulary associated with cockfighting can add the additional options of fighting cock and gamecock. Alternately, a more general approach offers another list of possibilities: chicken, bird, fowl, and animal. When combined, all of these variations reveal a rich semantic panorama that exists in English to describe Rulfo's world of raising, training, and fighting roosters. My version uses all of these options in an effort to avoid the redundancy that feels natural in Rulfo's original Spanish and yet awkward in English translation.

Finally, Rulfo's fascination with the regional fairs and festivals of central Mexico extends to the music that permeates these events and to the small mariachi bands and female balladeers who earn a hard-fought living on the road. As such, the novelist fills *The Golden Cockerel* with fragments of the melodies that *La Caponera* (and later her daughter) sings to animate the crowds. While the author invented some of these songs, others are authentic expressions of Mexico's popular music tradition. In both cases, Rulfo uses lyrics to mirror and reinforce the context of the scenes in which they appear. As such, I felt that the content of the musical selections was as important as their sound quality and I tried to emphasize both in my translation, but without a concern for recreating their strict poetic structure.

The "other writings" of this collection presented additional challenges. In particular and, as noted in the introduction, a few of these items are drafts that Rulfo never edited for publication. In my translation, I strove to retain some of the incomplete feel of these texts and a careful reader may find a few inconsistencies that the author likely would have changed on revision. One issue of particular note is a variation in the names that Rulfo uses for his protagonists in two stories. Don Tránsito in "Ángel Pinzón Paused," for example, is listed occasionally as Don Trinidad and

Don Procopio Argote as Don Toribio. Similarly, Candelario of "The Discoverer" abruptly becomes Catarino. The most likely explanation for these variations is Rulfo's tendency (mentioned in the introduction) to experiment with the names of his characters, trying out different labels before settling on a preferred option. Others might see this disparity as a nod to the fallibility of memory and oral narration. To avoid confusion for the casual reader, however, I have chosen to eliminate this vacillation (a decision that was also made for the Spanish-language version of this collection).

The reader who chooses to examine my translation against Rulfo's originals will, of course, discover other alterations that I adopted (mostly minor in nature). In each case, I was guided by the belief that a "faithful" translation often requires the translator to deviate from the more obvious literal option in favor of one that comes closer to the dynamic and creative feel of the original. In the end, like a sinner kneeling at the confessional, I take full responsibility for my choices, hoping that my efforts prove a worthy vessel for the first complete English-language version of the second novel of one of Latin America's most influential writers.

RULFO'S SECOND NOVEL:
THE GOLDEN COCKEREL

THE GOLDEN COCKEREL

THE MORNING WAS BREAKING.

Along the abandoned streets of San Miguel del Milagro, one or two shawl-covered women strolled toward the church, answering the call for first mass. A few others swept the dusty streets.

In the distance, far enough away that his words were imperceptible, one could hear the clamor of a crier. One of those town criers that go from street corner to street corner shouting the description of some lost animal, of a missing boy, or of a lost girl... In the case of the girl the account went further, since in addition to giving the date of her disappearance it was imperative to announce the likely culprit who had stolen her away, where she had been taken, and whether the parents wanted to object to or accept the arrangement. This was done to keep the town informed of what had happened and to shame the runaways into joining in matrimony... As for the lost animals, the crier would have to go out and search for them himself if announcing their loss came to naught, since otherwise no one would pay for the job.

As the women disappeared in the direction of the church, the crier's report could be heard even closer, until, stopped on some street corner and projecting his voice through his hands, he launched his shrill and quick-witted chants:

—Tan-colored sorrel... Of large stature... Five years old... Timid... Mark on its haunch... Branded on the same... Draw reigns... Wandered off the day before yesterday from the *Potrero Hondo*... Belongs to Don Secundino Colmenero. Twenty pesos reward to whoever finds him... No questions asked...

This last sentence was long and out of tune. After a while the crier walked a short way and repeated the same refrain, until the announcement faded and eventually dissolved into the farthest corners of the village.

The guy who plied this trade was Dionisio Pinzón, one of the poorest men of San Miguel del Milagro. He lived in a miserable shack on the edge of town in the company of his mother, an unwell and aged woman, more from want than from years. And even though the appearance of Dionisio Pinzón was that of a strong man, in truth he was disabled, with one of his arms disfigured, who knows just how. What's certain is that this made it impossible for him to complete some tasks, whether as a laborer or as a farmhand, the only occupations that were to be had in town. As such he was good for nothing, or at least that's how people saw him. And that's why he dedicated himself to the vocation of town crier, a trade that didn't require the use of his arms and that he completed quite well, since he had a voice and a willingness to do the job.

There was no corner of San Miguel del Milagro where he didn't shout his news, perhaps working on commission for some client or, if not, searching for the priest's scrawny cow that had the bad habit of bolting for the hills every time it discovered the gate to the parish corral open, something that happened all too often.

And even when there was no shortage of men out of work who, upon hearing the news, would offer to go in search of the aforementioned cow, there were times when Dionisio would take the task upon himself and receive for his efforts only a few blessings and the promise of collecting some payment in Heaven.

Through it all, whether he was paid or not, his voice never wavered and he just kept at it since, to be honest, what else could he do to keep from dying of hunger. And yet he didn't always make it home with his hands empty, like on this occasion when he had the job of announcing the loss of Don Secundino Colmenero's sorrel, from early in the morning until late at night, when it seemed that his yelling was blending with the barking of the dogs in the sleepy town. In any event, the horse had not turned up by the end of the day, nor was there anyone who could confirm its whereabouts; and Don Secundino wasn't going to pay up without first seeing his animal napping in the corral, not wanting to throw good money after bad. And yet, so that Dionisio Pinzón wouldn't become discouraged and stop announcing his loss, he gave him a tenth of a liter of beans as an advance that the crier wrapped in his scarf and carried home about midnight, which is when he arrived, burdened with hunger and fatigue. And like other times, his mother had managed to prepare him a bit of coffee and some *navegantes*, which weren't anything more than parboiled cactus leaves that at least served to fool his stomach.

But things weren't always so bad. Year after year, he was hired to announce the celebrations for the fair held in San Miguel. And that's where he could be found, out in front of the banging drums and the squealing oboe, where his pronouncements would take on a hollow sound as they were shouted through a cardboard megaphone, announcing card games, calf roping, cockfights, and, in passing, all of the church festivities for each day of the novena, without forgetting the exhibits of the traveling show or some unguent to cure all ills. Much further back in the parade that he was leading came the music of wind instruments that would liven up the moments when the crier rested by playing the discordant notes of a tune known as the "Zopilote Mojado." While trailing at the end of the procession were a number of carts that were adorned with young women all standing under arches made of reeds and soft cornstalks.

It was in these moments that Dionisio Pinzón would forget the privations that filled his life, since he marched quite content at the front of the proceedings, shouting to energize the clowns that strode by his side doing stunts and prancing about to entertain the public.

ONE OF THOSE YEARS, perhaps due to an abundant harvest or some unknown miracle, the rowdiest and best-attended festivities that anyone had seen in a long time were celebrated in San Miguel del Milagro. The excitement was so pervasive that two weeks later people were still contesting the card games, and the cockfights seemed to go on for so long that the region's cockfighters used up their supply of birds and still had time to order more animals, care for them, train them, and battle them. One of the owners who did this was Secundino Colmenero, the richest man in town, who ran out of his supply of fighting cocks and lost during these legendary matches, along with his money, a ranch that was full of hens and twenty-two cows that was all that he owned. And even though he recovered a bit in the end, he lost everything else in the never-ending wagers.

Dionisio Pinzón found himself hard pressed to complete so much work. At that moment not as a crier, but as an announcer in the cockfighting arena where he was able to monopolize almost all of the matches. Thus, in the last days, his voice sounded a bit fatigued, although he never failed to shout the Referee's commands at the top of his voice.

As it turns out, things were getting tense. The time had arrived when only the big names faced off, including some famous players who had come from the San Marcos Fair in Aguascalientes, as well as from Teocaltiche, Arandas, Chalchicomula, and Zacatecas, all sporting such fine roosters that it was a shame to see them perish. Also making an appearance were the singing divas who showed up from who knows where, attracted perhaps by the smell of money, since previously they had never come anywhere near San Miguel del Milagro, not even for a peek. At the front of them all was a tough and attractive woman with a flashy *rebozo* worn across her chest who they called *La Caponera*, perhaps on account of the sway she held over men. What's certain is that having these women here, singing their songs while surrounded by their mariachis, only added to the excitement of the cockfights.

The arena at San Miguel del Milagro was makeshift, without the capacity to hold large crowds. They used a corral at a brickyard for such events, where they raised a shanty that was partially covered with a straw-thatched roof. The ring was made of wooden boards while the benches that wrapped around it, and where the public would settle, were little more than planks laid on top of thick adobe bricks. Ultimately, this year things had become a bit complicated since no one could have imagined the arrival of such a large crowd. And, if that wasn't enough, at any moment a couple of *políticos* were expected to drop by. To accommodate them, the authorities ordered that the first two rows be cleared and that they remain empty until the arrival of those *señores* and even after that since, when push comes to shove, even though there were only two of them, each came with his own entourage of *pistoleros*. These men settled in the second row behind each corresponding boss, with the two main guys up front, facing each other but separated by the cockpit. And when the matches began it became evident that this pair of men, both sporting large sombreros, just didn't get along. They seemed to have shown up on account of some ancient rivalry that was evident not only in their personal attitudes but also in the very cockfights. If one of them took the side of a particular chicken, the other backed its opponent. And that's how tempers began to flare, since each wanted his own animal to win. It didn't take long for an altercation to occur: the loser jumped to his feet along with all of his associates, and that was the beginning of a chorus of obscenities and threats hurled back and forth between the opposing bands of hired guns. The spectacle of these two seemingly enraged gangs ended up holding the attention of the entire crowd since everyone expected a fight to break out between two men unwilling to pass on the opportunity to show how tough each was.

A few individuals didn't waste time abandoning the area out of fear that a gunfight would break out. But nothing happened. At the end of the match the two *políticos* left the arena. They met at the door. There they embraced and were later seen drinking together at a *canela* bar, along with the singers, the *pistoleros* who seemed to have forgotten their malice, and the *presidente municipal*, as if the whole of them were celebrating some pleasant chance encounter.

BUT GETTING BACK TO DIONISIO PINZÓN, it was on this felicitous night that the last cockfight of the evening changed his luck and amended his destiny.

A white rooster from Chicontepec was brought out to challenge a golden one from Chihuahua. The betting was fierce, so much so that someone with five thousand pesos bet it all and still wanted to go higher, putting it all on the cock from Chihuahua.

The white bird turned out to be timid. He showed fight when he was passed in front of his opponent, but when released on the line and facing the first lunges of the golden cockerel he bolted to one of the corners. And there he remained, with his head lowered and his wings wilted as if he were ill. At that, the gold-colored fowl went after the white one in search of a fight. He raised his hackles and stomped the ground hard as he circled the run-away bird. The bolter retreated even further against the barrier, showing his cowardice and, more than anything else, his desire to flee. But finding himself trapped by the bird from Chihuahua, he leapt in an attempt to get away from the attack and ended up falling on the sunflower-colored back of his enemy. He flapped his wings hard to keep his balance and, while hoping to get out of the jam in which he found himself, managed to break one of the golden cockerel's wings with the sharp blade attached to his spur.

The better rooster, now wounded and furious, charged his frightened opponent without mercy, sending him running for the corner where the trapped animal tried with little avail to make use of his limited ability to fly. This continued over and over again, until, unable to endure the loss of blood from his wound, the golden rooster dropped his beak and fell to the ground without the white chicken making even the slightest attempt to counterattack.

And that's how such a faint-hearted animal won the fight, and that's how Dionisio Pinzón called it when he shouted:

—It's all over folks! The favorite has lost!—followed closely by—: Oooopen the doors...!

The handler from Chihuahua grabbed the wounded bird. He blew into its beak hoping to clear any obstruction and tried to get the animal to stand on its own. Yet seeing that the chicken just kept falling down like a ball of feathers, he declared:

—Ain't nothing left to do but finish it off.

And he was ready to wring the bird's neck when Dionisio Pinzón dared to stop him:

—Don't kill him—he said—. He might get better and be worth something, even if only as a brood cock.

The man from Chihuahua laughed derisively and tossed the animal toward Dionisio Pinzón as if he were getting rid of a dirty rag. Dionisio caught him in midair, tucked him carefully in his arms, almost tenderly, and left the arena with his prize.

When he arrived home, he made a hole in the floor of his shack and, with the help of his mother, buried the rooster right there, leaving only the head exposed.

DAYS PASSED. Dionisio Pinzón spent all of his time thinking only about the fighting cock, which he pampered with care. He brought him water and food and placed small bits of tortilla and alfalfa leaves inside his beak trying to get him to eat. But the animal wasn't hungry, or thirsty; he seemed only to want to die, even though Dionisio was there to prevent just that by keeping a constant vigil over the drowsy bird that was half-buried in the ground.

Even so, one morning Dionisio faced a new problem. The cockerel wouldn't open his eyes and kept letting his neck droop under its own weight. As quick as he could, Dionisio placed a crate over the burial spot and beat on it with a rock for hours on end.

When he finally removed the box, the cock stared at him with a dazed look as the breath of resurrection flowed in and out of his partially open beak. Dionisio moved the water dish closer and the bird drank; he gave him corn paste to eat which he downed in a flash.

A few hours later, the cockerel was grazing in the full sun of the open pen. That golden chicken, still ashen from the dirt, and despite buckling every now and then without the support of his broken wing, showed signs of an exceptional nature by standing tall and sure in the face of life.

THE WING DIDN'T TAKE LONG TO HEAL EITHER. Although it ended up being a bit higher than its opposite, it flapped forcefully and its beat was brusque and defiant at the first light of each morning.

But about this time Dionisio Pinzón's mother passed away. It seemed as if she had traded in her life for that of the "crooked wing," as the golden cockerel ended up being called. As it turned out, while the latter kept getting better and better, the mother slowly bent over until she died, unwell from so much misfortune.

Year upon year of hardships, entire days of hunger and hopelessness had sent her to an early grave. And just now, when the son believed he had finally found the energy to fight strong for the two of them, the mother had neither the means nor the desire to regain her lost vigor.

The fact is that she died. And Dionisio Pinzón had to arrange the funeral without any money for a coffin to bury her in.

Perhaps that's when he began to hate San Miguel del Milagro. Not only because no one gave him a hand, but also because the town had gone so far as to mock him. Indeed, people laughed at the odd sight that Dionisio made as he marched down the middle of the road lugging on his shoulders some strange container that was made from the rotting boards of a door, while inside, wrapped in a *petate*, was the dead body of his mother.

Everyone who witnessed the spectacle sneered at Dionisio, believing that he must have been taking some dead animal to the dump.

To make things worse, and adding to the pain of his mother's demise, on that same day he had to announce the elopement of

Tomasa Leñero, the girl that he hoped to make his wife if poverty hadn't gotten in the way:

—Tomasa Leñero—he shouted—. Fourteen years old. Fled it would seem on the 24th as told by those who hang out with Miguel Tiscareño. Miguel, son of deceased parents. Tomasa, only daughter of Don Torcuato Leñero who begs to know where she's been taken.

And thus, with his double heartbreak, Dionisio Pinzón went from one street corner to the next until that point where the town dissolves into empty lots, shouting the news that ended up sounding more like a mournful lament than a simple announcement.

He rested on a large rock, exhausted after completing his rounds and there, with his face hardened into a resentful grimace, he promised that neither he nor any of his own would ever go hungry again…

The next day, at first light, Dionisio set off forever. He took with him only a small bundle of old clothes while, under his withered arm and shielded from the wind and the cold, was his golden rooster. And he headed out into the world determined to roll the dice with that *animalito*.

HE KNEW WHEN AND WHERE THE MATCHES TOOK PLACE through the connections he had developed with cockfighters while working as a town crier. And that's why one of the first places he visited was San Juan del Río. Destitute and ragged and still holding his bird in his arms, he headed to the cockpit to get his bearings and to see if he could find a *padrino* who could guarantee the bets on his behalf. He located one, but not for that afternoon, since all of the current fights were scheduled matches. He had to wait until the next day for the open class battles that would begin at eleven in the morning. And with that delay, he spent the night at the inn, with his cockerel tethered to the legs of his cot, never shutting his eyes out of fear that someone might pilfer the animal in which he had placed all of his hopes.

He spent the few centavos he had to feed the bird, giving him a small bit of chopped meat that he mixed with some mirasol chiles. That's what he gave him for dinner and then again for breakfast when he got up the next morning.

When the eleven o'clock fights started up, he was already there, next to the guy who was going to sponsor him, one of those professional gamblers who if you win will take eighty percent of the earnings and if you lose will say goodbye to his money and Dionisio Pinzón to his cockerel. That's how the deal was made.

The morning fights never attract real cockfighters, and the crowds at the ring are made up mostly of the curious and gawkers who don't risk in their betting as much as the animals are worth. That's why most of the birds are of a low grade.

Even so, you could win a little something if you were to win at all. And Dionisio Pinzón won. His rooster didn't lose a single feather and ended the match with his metal spur bloodied all the way to the binding.

After that, his *padrino*, while handing over the few pesos that belonged to him, told Dionisio that his bird was too much rooster to fight against those hens, and he made an effort to convince him to try his luck in the main events, even going so far as accepting a lesser role in the partnership, indicating that he would take it upon himself to find a challenger. Dionisio agreed, after all that's why he had shown up, to test the mettle of his gamecock, an animal in which he placed more faith than he had ever had in any person.

By the afternoon, the arena was entirely different. The best seats of each section were filled with high-society types. Singers performed on the stage and throughout the packed arena you could feel the enthusiasm and joy in the air. When it was Dionisio Pinzón's turn, they weighed his bird on the scale. With its head covered, since that's what had been required by the challenger who also demanded the right to select the spurs and even the person to attach them. Dionisio assumed that this was because he was going up against an owner looking for some kind of advantage. But he didn't have any recourse other than to accept these conditions, unless he was willing to let someone else pit his rooster, which he wasn't, since he didn't want anyone to have the chance to injure his animal. So he was at least allowed that one concession.

Finally they threw out a dark-red bird, almost black, that began strutting around the ring to show off its poise, glancing here and there just like a bull that has been released from the pen and is searching for its adversary.

—Aa-tention!—yelled the announcer—: San Juan del Río against San Miguel del Milagro! Let's start the betting off even! At one hundred pesos!

—Eighty! Eighty on the red one!

—I'll pay seventy! Seventy! I'm going for San Juan del Río!

Dionisio Pinzón took his golden cockerel from the flour sack where the half-dazed bird had been wrapped and led him for just a moment around the edge of the pit.

The betting went quickly against him:

—Sixty! Fifty! It's at one hundred to fifty!

The runners bounced around the plaza grabbing the bets from here and there, all the while yelling:

—One hundred to fifty! Tell me which one you want!

Dionisio Pinzón smiled as he saw that the wagers in his favor were going lower and as the confused shouts of those who only wanted to put money on the bird from San Juan del Río made it all the way down to him. He tried to locate his *padrino* among the crowd, but when he couldn't see him anywhere he simply caressed his bird and combed its feathers.

—Take them off, *señores!*—the judge ordered from his seat.

They removed the leather covers from the spurs. Both challengers placed their fighting cocks on the line and when they heard the command to pit, they pitted the birds. The other guy ended up with a few feathers in his hand that he had ripped from his animal at the last minute in an attempt to get it mad, while Dionisio Pinzón released his gently on the line.

Everything went silent.

Not three minutes had passed when a gasp of dismay spread through the crowd. The dark-red chicken lay sprawled on the ground, on its side, kicking out its agony. The golden bird had finished it off cleanly, almost inexplicably, and was still beating his wings and crowing to provoke his adversary.

Dionisio picked up the animal before he could hurt himself with the enormous metal spur. He crossed the pit to the jeering of the angry crowd and placed the blade on the judge's table. Only the sweeper, who entered to remove the dead bird's blood with his broom, offered any words of appreciation:

—You got a bird that could thrash any of them, amigo. He knows how to fight.

—Yep... He knows how to fight—was Dionisio's response, as he left in search of his *padrino*. He found him in the cantina.

—Did you collect the winnings?

—The truth is I came over here a bit early to get a drink and calm my nerves. I figured your bird was gonna get thumped. And how the hell was I gonna cover the bets.

—You had so little faith in my *animalito*?

—It's just I never imagined that Don So-and-So, the guy I made the deal with, was gonna throw in his red and black rooster, that to tell you the honest-to-God truth was a killer... He always held him back for the fights at San Marcos... He's always won big with that one.

—And yet he still wanted an advantage.

—So you see. That'd spook anyone. And then when I saw how the betting was going against us... I panicked, like anyone would.

—But we weren't there to lose. You had to know that.

—How could I have known? That's why I figured it was better to hide out here... Just in case.

—So I would've been strung up if we'dve lost?

—More or less... At the end of the day you ain't got much to lose. I, on the other hand... Try to understand that this is how I make my living... Anyway, what're we bitching about now? Let's go collect—he said while pouring one last drink.

Later the two of them headed toward the cashier; but by that time another fight had begun and they had to wait for it to finish. All of a sudden one could hear the followers of the winning bird yelling ¡*Viva Tequisquiapan!*, while from up on the stage the singers took it upon themselves to fill the interval with their singing. Dionisio Pinzón, while waiting for his *padrino* to return, got a long look at these women, especially at the one out front whom he was sure he already knew. He nudged his way closer until he was at the edge of the platform where he could study her while she belted out the words to her song:

> *Last night I dreamt that I loved you,*
> *like one does only once in a lifetime;*
> *I woke and found that all was a lie*
> *and no longer remember who you are...*

—It's done—the *padrino* declared, showing him the money he had collected.

—Who's that woman singing? I think I've seen her somewhere before.

—They call her *La Caponera*. And her calling is to wander the earth, so it's not hard to have seen her just about anywhere... ¡*Vámonos!*

> *... If I loved you it's not that I loved you,*
> *if I adored you, it was simply to pass the time,*
> *and now I return your unhappy portrait*
> *for nothing to remind me of you...*

WITH THE MONEY EARNED IN SAN JUAN DEL RÍO he was able to travel farther abroad. And he set out on the road to Zacatecas, where he was told the gaming was good. The man who had served as his *padrino* took it upon himself to tag along, even though Dionisio Pinzón preferred to go at it alone, since in their short time together he had already learned the tricks of the trade and it was clear, although the guy's advice might be of some use, that he was the type who was only out for himself. And from then on Dionisio wanted whatever he earned to be his alone.

Who can say how many towns he traveled through during those days; what's certain is that when he arrived in Aguascalientes, on his way to the San Marcos Fair, his bird was still with him and very much alive. And yet Dionisio was different: his attire showed that he was in mourning, and that's how he would dress until the day he died.

This was the first time that Dionisio had come anywhere close to Aguascalientes. He arrived excited to see if his cockerel really could match up against the finest animals that would be fought here, seeing as none were entered, and that was according to the rules, except those considered to be of *Brava Ley* or *Ley Suprema*; those that are given the first title are quick to attack, while those declared to be *Ley Suprema* are persistent fighters who throw solid jabs and display courage up to the last moments of their lives. And what Dionisio Pinzón wanted was to know what kind of bird he had so he signed it up to be the *Mochiller* on the second day of the fights, the *Mochiller* being the first chicken to be put into play and that, to distinguish it from the others, is given a larger sum of money.

It was here in Aguascalientes that he again ran into his *padrino* from San Juan del Río. But this time the guy didn't seem at all excited to help, since he didn't consider Dionisio Pinzón to be a good bet against the truly experienced cockfighters that would show up for the San Marcos Fair. And that wasn't all, since on their first opportunity to converse the *padrino* told him:

—You'd be better off hitting the small town circuit with this runt of a bird, here they're gonna fleece you.

—When it comes down to it, I've got nothing to lose. Ain't that what you told me?

—Perhaps the few thousand pesos that you must've won on the road...Just know that lady luck doesn't travel on the back of a burro.

—That's why I didn't want to stick with you—countered Dionisio. And they went their separate ways never to see each other again.

With the applause for the singing divas still thundering throughout the arena and, with the announcer declaring the beginning of the afternoon fights, Dionisio Pinzón found himself breasting his golden cockerel in front of a prancing black rooster that was speckled with white spots. He could clearly hear the nature of the betting and how little by little things were going against him and in favor of his rival, although there was also a scattering of counter wagers, bets that were placed perhaps by onlookers who were already bored or uninformed, making him a bit worried. Yet when he noticed that the opposing handler was stressing his bird and irritating it with slaps to the head he knew that he was going to win the fight since his gold-colored chicken, accustomed to being treated well, knew how to fight cleanly and could easily placate angry opponents.

And that's what happened. As the spotted bird strutted around, the golden cockerel was not fooled by its bouncing head and launched an attack from the side, blade against blade, throwing himself at the other's breast and pulling at him with his legs. The adversary bobbed his head, like a boxer while sparring, but he left his body almost motionless. And it was there, in the rump, where the golden rooster buried his spur, crippling his rival and leaving him dazed and looking for any place to thrust his beak.

—Death Blow!—roared the announcer—. Nochistlán loses! Everyone satisfied! Ooo-pen the doors!

... Behind bars in Celaya
without sin was I kept,
for a wretched little pitaya
that my little bird pecked;
oh what a story they told,
for that cut was already old...

The spirited tune that the singers used to break the tension, along with the grumbling of the arena, tasted just like glory to Dionisio Pinzón as he recovered his bird that, although spattered with blood, was whole and once again uninjured.

—HEY, COCKFIGHTER!—he heard someone call out to him. He had decided to eat roasted chicken in one of the booths at the fair. His bird was already safely put away and he had wandered around curiously inspecting the event's many sights. Now he was waiting for his meal to be served.

He turned his head and noticed the imposing figure of a *charro* staring down at him from above.

—You need something?—Dionisio Pinzón asked.

—How much would you take for your bird?

—He's not for sale.

—I'll give you a thousand pesos but don't tell anyone you sold him to me.

—I'm not gonna sell.

The *charro* approached Dionisio Pinzón and offered his hand as an introduction. Tagging along, but unseen until just now when she stepped into the light, was *La Caponera*, the same stunning woman who had been singing in the arena.

—The name's Lorenzo Benavides. Haven't you ever heard of Don Lorenzo Benavides? Well there you go, that's me. I'm also the owner of the spotted bird that was wounded earlier this afternoon by your animal. I'll offer you one thousand five hundred pesos for him with the only condition being that you don't let anyone know you gave him to me...

—I already told you he ain't for sale.

—...One more thing—the man named Lorenzo Benavides continued, without paying any attention to Dionisio Pinzón's response—, I'll give you two thousand pesos as well as two yellow roosters just like the one you've got. Real nice birds. That in your hands... And by God I believe you've got a good touch!, could win it all wherever you decide to take them... And another thing...

—I ain't interested in your offer. Want to join me for supper?

—What?

—I asked if you wanted some chicken.

—No, thanks. I never eat chicken... And certainly not during cockfighting season... So you up to making a deal?... Listen to me good, cockfighter—he said taking on a serious tone—. You're not gonna be able to fight that little bird around here again. People are on to him and know what he can do. And if you go ahead, they'll send out a rooster that'll give him his *golpe de gracia* in the first blows... And one more thing...

—I'm not planning on fighting him for now.

—...One more thing, as I was saying, that's how it'll go down if you're the one who pits him. But if it's me, that bird'll be in the arena tomorrow morning, competing with a three to two advantage or maybe even five to one. That's if they believe the animal's from my coop. Otherwise... Even I have a bird that can take yours. So you'll see.

—Take the deal, cockfighter. It's for the best—intervened *La Caponera*, who for the last while had been seated in front of Dionisio Pinzón—. Or don't you understand the arrangement that Don Lorenzo is proposing?

—I understand. I just don't like scams.

She responded with a boisterous laugh. And then continued:

—It's clear as day that you know nothing about this kind of a thing. When you've been around a bit longer you'll know that anything goes when it comes to cockfighting.

—Well, up to now I've won straight up. So... if you'll excuse me—said Dionisio Pinzón seeming somewhat offended. Considering the matter closed he turned his attention to finishing his meal.

La Caponera shrugged her shoulders. She got up from the table and, along with Lorenzo Benavides, made her way to a different spot, but not far away.

—What you gonna drink, Bernarda?—he heard Benavides ask the woman.

—Well for the moment have them bring a couple of cervezas, don't you think?

—And how about a bit of *mezcal* first to make the beer go down better.

—Sounds good.

The waiter came over and they asked him for a bottle of *mezcal*. From where he sat, and while taking care of his meal, Dionisio Pinzón kept an eye on the pair. Especially the woman, that beautiful woman!, who drank one shot of *mezcal* after another and laughed and laughed eagerly at everything Lorenzo Benavides said. Meanwhile, Pinzón studied the happy sparkle of eyes that were set within an extraordinarily pretty face. And he suspected, on account of the shape of her arms and her breasts, covered by a white *rebozo* that hung across her body, that her figure must be beautiful as well. She was wearing a low-cut blouse and a black skirt embossed with red tulips.

From one bite to the next, he never took his eyes off that woman who had spoken up in support of the deal put forward by Lorenzo Benavides, a man whose appearance made it clear that he must be some famous owner of fighting cocks.

Dionisio finished eating and got up. Before leaving, he bid farewell to the occupants of the next table over, who didn't seem to hear him. The guy was too engrossed in his own story, perhaps trying to convince the lady of something. And she didn't take her eyes off of him, offering a gaze that was by then a bit glassy due to the *mezcal* that she continued drinking in excess.

TWO MONTHS LATER Dionisio's golden cockerel was killed in Tlaquepaque.

From the opening moments of the contest it was clear that his bird was facing an adversary that was born to kill. It was a beautiful animal. Very fine, with a black and white coat and a huge ruff full of feathers and, above all else, an eagle-like gaze with eyes reddened by a rage that surely wouldn't be tamed until the death of that unfortunate gold-colored fighting cock.

As the two birds were breasted, the opponent was so quick to attack that Dionisio Pinzón didn't have time to free his animal, which began to bleed at the comb from the violent and brutal strikes that the black and white bird landed in just a matter of seconds.

—I'll take one hundred to fifty! I'm going for that black and white bird!—cried the bettors.

And like an echo, the bookies repeated:

—One hundred to fifty! On the favorite! Keep bidding *señores*! One hundred to fifty! Who else wants the black and white bird?

—I'll go with forty! I'll do a hundred to forty!

The blood flowing from the golden cockerel's comb began to drop into his nostrils making him struggle for air. Dionisio Pinzón wiped off the bird's head and blew into his beak to clear everything out. He took some dirt from the ground and rubbed it into the animal's comb hoping to stop the bleeding and, something that he had never done before, he began stressing the rooster by pulling feathers from his tail to provoke him. Thus, when the call came to: Pit your birds, *señores!*, the golden cockerel, fighting mad, didn't drop easily to the line, but rather seemed to flee from Dionisio Pinzón's hands and ran straight into the black and white chicken that stopped him cold by leaping in mid-air and throwing its feet out front. The challenger then seized him by the beak and shook until, after a number of feints and flaps of its wings, it climbed on top of the golden cockerel, bruised his head with jabs from its beak, and buried the blade of the spur into his chest. The gold-colored bird ended up with his legs in the air, slashing wildly, but by now in his last moments of life.

—Recover your birds, *señores!*

By tradition and by rule, the judge demanded proof that the contest was over. Dionisio raised his animal and passed him in front of the black and white bird, which began to peck fiercely at the bloodstained comb of the golden rooster, that, as everyone could see, was by then quite dead.

DIONISIO PINZÓN abandoned the arena carrying in his hands just a few feathers and a keepsake of blood. Outside was the roar of the fair: the amusements, the promotions for games of chance going on inside the various tents, the hollering of the guy paid to announce the lottery and roulette matches, the muffled voices of the card and the dart players, and the crafty chatter of those who challenged any onlooker to guess where the tiny ball had ended up. All the while he could still sense the din of the cockpit, the stench of smoke and alcohol that obscured the scent of blood that was scattered all over the ground, and the smell of dead roosters, deboned and hanging by a hook. And the shouts of a fevered crowd: That one's a do-nothing! He's a coward! ¡*Viva Quitupan*!, were in turn drowned out by the voices of the singers that competed with the hollow strings of the *tololoche*. And all of that was mixed in with the confused shouting of the merchants, the gamblers, and the traveling musicians.

He was brought back to reality by the sound of dice rattling in a tumbler and then rolling across green flannel. Back inside, the arena had returned to silence with the end of the intermission that separated his match from the one that was just now getting underway.

He wandered a few steps and paused in front of the card tables.

—Stop shuffling like that 'cause people can see the cards!—he heard someone tell the dealer from among those who were clustered around one of the tables.

Dionisio Pinzón lingered awhile, without any intention of playing, just nosing around. He had almost no money left, just enough to pay for a meal and lodging for that night, since his gamecock had taken with him in death what the *animalito* had won for him in the previous months. The truth of the matter was that he had no idea what to do or where to go; that's why he stood there gawking, imagining himself betting everything on the cards that the dealer dealt on the table and winning or losing the hand all in his imagination. Finally, he was ready to commit. He took his money from the belt where he had it stashed and played it on a Page of Coins that was pared with an Ace of Cups.

—I like Coins—he said, and placed his pesos one by one on the Page.

The cards were dealt, slowly, deliberately. The dealer, with each card, raised the deck up high:

—Seven of Cups—he would say—. Two of Coins. Five of Clubs. King of Clubs. Four of Swords. Knight of Coins. And... Ace of Clubs—he kept dealing the rest of the cards, naming each one quickly—: Two, Five, Three, Page, Page. You almost had it, *señor*.

Dionisio Pinzón watched as they picked up his money. He stepped back a bit to make room for others, while the banker cried out:

—In the next one you'll find your luck! Place your bets where you want them, *señores*! Here we go!

He didn't want to leave right away to avoid the appearance that he was fleeing. And when he finally got the courage to exit he found himself face to face with the glowing image of *La Caponera*, all decked out in an ample poppy-flowered dress with a *rebozo* folded like a cartridge belt across her chest.

She took a colored handkerchief from her bosom that was filled with a good fistful of pesos all rolled up and, without undoing it, offered it to Dionisio:

—Listen up, cockfighter, I want you to bet these centavos on that Six of Clubs sitting there next to the Knight of Coins.

—And what do you care, Doña Bernarda?... My luck's shot. You saw it yourself. Or what, you just out to waste your money?

—I know what I'm doing. Just play them for me!

—Here it goes, but it's on you... 'Cause I'd sooner go for the Knight.

—Well put it on the Knight... If it makes you feel better, I mean.

Dionisio Pinzón stared at her as if trying to guess the intentions of her words and, without taking his eyes off her malicious smile, he let the bundle drop, covering the Six of Clubs.

—Just remember that I ain't responsible.

—Don't worry, cockfighter... And don't feel bad.

The dealer began to throw out the cards and on the third try the Six of Clubs popped up.

—Six is a winner, with a little help from your "old lady"!—yelled the dealer.

The banker undid the knot in the handkerchief. He counted up the money that was kept inside and paid its equivalent plus another half of the same.

—Here's your "old lady's" take—he said.

—Gather it up!—*La Caponera* told Pinzón.

He collected the pile of pesos and, without touching what was inside the handkerchief, tied it back up and returned it to *La Caponera*, who let it disappear into her bosom.

—Now to the cockfights, let's see if you ain't back on your game.

—I'm not up to playing with someone else's dough.

—I got my own money right here—said *La Caponera* clutching her chest—. So don't you worry about it... And, by the way, after the cockfights I want a word with you.

The malicious smile returned to her face. And then she added:

—Me and another guy.

The pair headed off toward the arena. But before entering he held her back to ask:

—Tell me, Doña Bernarda. You've gotta have some kind of a deal with the guy back at the tables, no? I clearly saw the Knight when the dealer cut the cards.

—Don't ever believe what you see. These guys always work with marked cards.

And without another word, the two entered the arena. While Dionisio Pinzón looked for an empty place to sit, she made her way up to the stage and began to sing:

Pretty little pitaya flower
white flower of the garambullo
I am quite so full of pride
for where I go, who can follow?
And even though you see me leave
my heart remains with you.

The woodpecker when in the wild
is quite quick to get to work,
and when he there finds a hole
with his beak he fills it full.
The woodpecker and I are quite alike
especially when my girl is near.

Oh!, how my haunch is sore
Oh!, how my strap pulls tight.
Let's see now if I clear this hurdle
only later to swell from the shock
for when in sight of so many fillies

I only neigh for the one that's mine.

Now I am a sparrowhawk
with full color in my wings;
truly I am not afraid to dream
nor will I off guard be caught
while I speak with the one I love;
even though by the knife I die…

And so it was in Tlaquepaque where he really got to know who Bernarda Cutiño was, a woman he had contemplated so many times before without seeking her attention nor much less her friendship. And although she had offered him advice in Aguascalientes, that was certainly no reason to believe he could one day be deserving of her; rather, he imagined that he had fallen out of her favor.

Bernarda Cutiño was a singer of certain renown, so full of drive and daring that when she sang she would get the crowd worked up, although she was never the type to let anyone paw at her, and if someone did go after her she would become surly and behave badly. Strong, beautiful, outgoing, and, above all, shrewdly mutable, offering her friendship to those who could prove themselves loyal. She had eyes of lightening, always moist, and a gravelly voice. Her body was nimble, firm, and when she raised her arms her breasts would try to break free of her bodice. She always wore spacious skirts of printed percale, with loud colors and full of pleats, which she finished off with a silken *rebozo* and flowers in her braids. From her neck she dangled strings of coral and necklaces made of colored beads; she kept her arms crowded with bracelets and her ears with large rings or oversized gold pendants. She was a woman with a strong temperament who wore a pleasant countenance wherever she went, something that served her well as a singer of *corridos* and old-style songs.

As far as anyone could tell, since her days as a small child *La Caponera* had roamed from town to town in the company of her mother, a poor wanderer in search of festivals, up until that moment when, with her mother dead from a fire in one of the tents, she came to rely on her own wits, joining up with one of those groups of traveling musicians who just take to the road attentive to whatever Providence might decide to send their way.

The "other guy" that *La Caponera* had mentioned was none other than the same Lorenzo Benavides who had tried to buy his bird in Aguascalientes.

The three of them sat on a long bench in front of a table covered with salsas and plates full of onion, lime, and oregano. While waiting to be served the cervezas that they had ordered, Lorenzo rambled on:

—Look here, Pinzón, this little game of cockfighting has its secrets. It can make you rich or send you to hell along with all of your money. If you had listened to us in Aguascalientes none of this would've happened to you.

—It was just my bird's time. The fight was legit from what I saw.

—Then can you tell me why your chicken was lame? That was clear from the get-go. They messed with your bird, that's what happened.

—And who'd be able to pull a stunt like that on me? I didn't let that animal out of my sight for even a moment.

—Perhaps it was at the weigh-in, Benavides told him, some dirty handler with quick fingers could've buried a fingernail into your bird without you seeing a thing. Some people are willing to do anything.

—But the animal fought bravely. He wouldn't have gone so hard if he'd been hurt.

—Because he was in good shape... But that can't change the fact that he was lame. I saw it.

They brought out the cervezas and a few plates full of something steaming. But Dionisio Pinzón pushed his drink to the side.

—Would you prefer something stronger? They've got some of the best tequila here—Benavides said.

—No. I'm not in the habit of drinking—Dionisio responded.

—Great, all the better for our plans. Look, as I was saying just now, when it comes to fighting roosters a lone guy hasn't got a chance. Look at me, I'm good and rich and I owe it all to those little birds. Yep. And to something else. My connections with other cockfighters, our arrangements, or dirty tricks if you will. But not making a fuss about it like you did just now.

—What are you getting at, if I'm allowed to ask? I've already lost and I'm outta here.

—And what you gonna do? You gonna go out and sell enchiladas? No, mi amigo Pinzón, you've caught the bug and you ain't gonna give up cockfighting.

—Ain't got nothing to keep me around here. No bird, no money... And there's more than enough gawkers. I'm headed back to my *pueblo*.

—What'd you do back there, if that ain't too much to ask?

—I worked... I got by.

—You got by starving to death. I've gotta tell you. I know how to size people up with just a quick glance. And you're one of those, forgive me for saying so, one of those that don't want nothing to do with hard work... No Pinzón, you're like me. Hard work ain't for us, that's why we're looking for an easier vocation. And what's better than gaming, where we sit around waiting for luck to take care of us.

—Maybe you're right. But as I said before, what are you getting at?

—That's where I'm headed...

with another round of cervezas and picked up Dionisio's empty plates, since while they conversed Bernarda Cutiño had been taking care of the drinks, Pinzón had been eating, and Benavides speaking. There's probably no need pointing out that Bernarda Cutiño had consumed all of the beer by herself, that she was now working on refilling her glass, and that her eyes had already taken on that half-asleep look that booze gives you. That's why her voice stammered when she joined the conversation:

—Lorenzo—she said—, let me explain to our amigo here what this is all about. You always go on and on without getting anywhere.

—Go on, then.

And she began to explain:

—Lorenzo wants you to throw in with him for the rest of the season. You'll register his birds in your name and you'll work for him as his handler. The deal is that you gotta do whatever he says. So you see, we're talking about pulling a fast one: you gotta break

the animal's ribs before pitting it, 'cause when the ribs are broken...
It's what everyone does, so he ain't asking you to do nothing out
of the ordinary.

—But why's it gotta to be me, seeing as there're so many other
handlers that could pull that off.

—Well, for the same reason as always, 'cause you have to pick
someone, right?

—And you've found your chump in me, is that it?

She emptied her glass before responding:

—No, Pinzón, it's nothing against you... Look, I can never
remember the face of a stranger... One of those cocky guys who
gets into the arena without any real idea of what he's doing...

Dionisio Pinzón made an effort to get up and leave the woman
to her ramblings, since it was quite clear that the beer had gone
to her head and was pushing her to say such harsh things, almost
offensive. But she grabbed his arm and forced him back into his
seat, while changing the expression on her face to smile at him
with her eyes:

—Let me finish—she told him—. What we were saying is that
no one knows you around here nor do they take you seriously.
That plays in your favor. The idea is that you'll pit Lorenzo's birds
as if they were your own and dupe the bettors. You get it, right?...
No, you don't get it.

—The fact is I understand all too well.

—Another thing—intervened Lorenzo Benavides—. Tomorrow
I'll take you to see my birds and I'll show you which one will go
up against the other, so you'll know which one to fight to lose and
which one to win. Don't you worry about the results, since I'll bid

how I see fit. Sleep on it tonight and tomorrow early we'll talk.

They took their leave, but by the next day Dionisio had agreed to a deal that promised solid winnings without any risk of his own. The scheme was similar to the one offered in Aguascalientes that he had refused, more out of honor than some ignorance about the ways of seasoned gamblers. He already knew back then, that in the business of cockfighting, it's not always the best or the most valiant that comes out on top and that, despite the rules, handlers have all kinds of tactics and gadgets they can use to cheat without ever getting caught.

Now he was going to fight cocks from the same coop, while knowing beforehand which one held the advantage. All of them were fine birds, haughty and proud, although each had its equal. All of them would face off in arranged matches that would be both safe and already won, if not in the pit then certainly in the betting. Lorenzo Benavides, by bidding hard, would force those who were keeping an eye on him to do the same, going along with him or against him, since no one could dispute his knowledge of the game.

Of the three birds that Dionisio Pinzón pitted that first afternoon he picked only one back up alive. On the second afternoon he gave a beating to his opponents in all three fights. He sat out one day and returned to the arena on the fourth, only to find that his animals weren't even good enough for the henhouse, since each one ended up hanging from the hooks where dead birds are left to draw out their last drops of blood. On the fifth day, and the last one of the scheduled fights, he sent the arena into an uproar when he won big with a sightless bird that, nonetheless, dealt blows that landed like a blind-man's cane on a heavy and cowardly rooster that sported the pompous name of Santa Gertrudis. Betting went against the blind bird and dropped from one thousand to seven hundred pesos and later to the amount of several thousand against one thousand pesos.

At the sound of "It's all over folks" the arena erupted in shouts of disgust and protest. But the judge had already made his decision and the announcer repeated the call:

—It's all over folks! That's it for Santa Gertrudis!

A few who had seen the expected winner as a sure thing had wagered everything, even the shirts off their backs. And, had they brought their women along, they would have risked them against the blind challenger as well.

What happened was that Lorenzo Benavides's men were scattered among the various sections of the arena, flaunting false looks of resignation and defeat, while enduring bids of eighty, of eight hundred, of one thousand against one thousand five hundred. Lorenzo was ecstatic, but pretended to be indifferent, as if he weren't concerned about the results or the support that just about everyone showed for his bird. Meanwhile, Dionisio Pinzón, with his cataract-riddled animal, acted as if he didn't hear the screams of: Make him wear glasses! Take him straight to the slaughterhouse! Show him the door!

The shouting from the spectators only got worse when the rooster was breasted in front of his opponent since the cockerel, sensing his enemy's presence, began striking at the air. But when released, the blind animal went furiously after his competitor that was oversized at more than four kilos, and, perhaps smelling his rival, refused to let go of its lumbering body, which he shredded with the dagger that was attached to his spur. And even after the other bird fell to the ground mortally wounded, the blind animal continued battering it with his wings and his beak while throwing withering knife-blows.

Dionisio Pinzón set out to collect his rooster that was still perched on top of the now dead adversary, viciously cutting at him; but someone from the audience, wearing a *tejana* hat and carrying a pistol, jumped into the ring. Before Dionisio could protect his animal, the guy snatched him up, shook him furiously, wrung his neck by spinning him around in circles like a pinwheel, and finally threw him into the angry crowd.

To protest the outrage Dionisio Pinzón asked the judge for and was granted permission to withdraw from the remaining matches.

Not long after that, Dionisio traveled with Lorenzo Benavides to the latter's home of Santa Gertrudis where he had been invited to spend a few days. There the pair celebrated their exploits with the blind rooster and laughed about how seriously they had taken the whole incident.

The two weeks that he spent at Santa Gertrudis were profitable ones. He learned, first by watching and then by joining in, just how to play *Paco Grande*, a card game that's a bit complicated, but engaging, and that distracted both men from the boredom of that isolated and solitary location.

Dionisio Pinzón proved capable and adapted easily to any game, something that he would later use to his advantage while accumulating an immense fortune. But at that moment he was still partial to the soft, silky, and brightly colored gamecocks that he would soon own in abundance. It didn't take long for Dionisio to stop being that humble man that we had known in San Miguel del Milagro, who, having at first only one bird as his entire fortune, always appeared restless and nervous and, scared of losing, always commended himself to the Lord before competing. Yet, little by little, his very nature was becoming something else through his exposure to the violent sport of cockfighting, as if the thick, reddish liquid coming from those dying animals had turned him to stone, transforming him into a cold and calculating man, sure and confident in the path of his destiny.

When he returned to San Miguel del Milagro, Dionisio was a different person than the one everyone there had known. He showed up just as the festival at San Miguel was getting started, barely a year and eight months after he had abandoned the town with the idea of never coming back. But as it was discovered, and according to what he claimed, he was not home to participate in the grand celebration, but rather to lay his mother to rest who, as it just so happens, was already in the ground.

—But poorly buried!—he replied to the mayor, who tried to make the situation clear—. And now I'm back to give her a respectable burial, just as she deserves.

He had with him a very nice casket that he had ordered especially for the occasion in San Luis Potosí, lined on the inside with satin and on the outside with purple velvet, and decorated with a molding made of pure silver.

—At least in death I want her to enjoy the rest and comfort she never knew in life.

But neither the town's priest nor its mayor was willing to let him open the grave:

—After five years have past—they told him—you can exhume your mother's cadaver... Before then, there's no way.

—I'm gonna do it right now. That's why I'm back... Even if I have to bribe the authorities to make it happen. Even if I have to pay someone off to get the permits—he added while looking straight at the priest—, anybody.

And he would have done just that except that when he showed up at the cemetery where his mother was buried, accompanied by a few *peones* armed with picks and shovels, he couldn't find the exact spot where he had laid his mother since there weren't any mounds or crosses, just an open field full of weeds.

In the few days that he lingered, people noticed the contempt that he felt for the town, for he was behaving like a bad-tempered and conceited loudmouth. And perhaps to remember times that weren't all that long in the past, he took advantage of the moment of the banquet to place himself in front of everyone, although in a way that was quite different from how he had done so previously, seeing as this time he stood before the *charros* and the musicians as if he were going to pay all of the expenses of the feast.

On top of that, he spoke to no one and treated with obvious contempt anyone who tried to get close enough to say hello. The one exception was Secundino Colmenero, with whom he had a long heart-to-heart hoping to bring him along to castrate and pit his gamecocks.

Colmenero, although fretting about having to leave his home and the few belongings that he still possessed, opted in the end to set out with Dionisio Pinzón because, to tell the truth, it had been more than a year since he lost his fortune gambling and he hadn't yet been able to get his life back on track. Faced with the opportunity of taking charge of all of Dionisio Pinzón's roosters and of being the one responsible for fighting those animals, he consented. After all, he enjoyed the business, he would be able to care for that whole coop of fine birds as if they were his own, and he would travel with them from one fair to another.

With that the two men abandoned San Miguel del Milagro to never return. And because the town was still celebrating, the pair marched into oblivion amid the ringing of church bells, along streets adorned with wreaths of flowers, and following behind a strange cross-like shape that was created by a casket and the animal that carried it.

Meanwhile, *La Caponera* passed the time waiting for Dionisio Pinzón in a village called Nochistlán, home to the area's annual fair. She hadn't accompanied Dionisio to San Miguel del Milagro because, as always, she was the one responsible for filling the arena with her songs.

That the two of them would join forces to face the difficult world of festival life together was a decision that had been made months earlier, when the pair ran into each other again at a place called Cuquío. They hadn't been in touch since those eventful days at Tlaquepaque, where Pinzón had lost his golden cockerel but had gained the friendship of Lorenzo Benavides, an alliance that would boost his own luck. And from there things had only gotten better. He not only learned a good deal about the profession, but was also set up with a fine bunch of birds that made him excited to get back into the game.

Cuquío was a small place, but one that was plagued with gamblers, crooks, cockfighters, and folk that would spend their time saving every little bit of money during the entire year just to go and throw it at the feet of some animal or lose it by betting against marked cards. The reputation of the town as a place to squander one's cash was such that you could get in on a game of *Brisca, Conquián, Siete y Medio,* or *Paco* not only in the area officially sanctioned for gambling but also in any cantina, shop, drugstore, or even on any of the benches of the main plaza. And if somebody ended up dead, and there were always a few, it was due to brawls caused by the games, since there was very little consumption of alcohol. And so it was that Dionisio Pinzón and *La Caponera* happened upon each other again in this small town and in this environment.

After tethering his birds to stakes in the pen at the arena and leaving them in the care of a trusted worker, he set off to take a turn around town. It didn't take him long to notice that everyone was so engrossed in the card games, encircling the players or taking part in the betting, that, despite the swarming crowds, there was a silence that seemed to dominate the place. He headed toward the largest event, where the commotion was the most pronounced and where you could hear the music from the mariachis.

That's where he found *La Caponera,* belting out a *corrido* from on top of the roulette table, although her voice sounded a bit faint due to the buzzing of so many people and the lack of any good way to capture her song under the roof of that makeshift structure that was open to the four winds.

Dionisio Pinzón waited for the song to end and then made his way over to her to say hello. They were both happy to see each other again; so much so, that she placed her arms tenderly around him while he held her in his for quite a while.

—Look at that. We're having such good weather even an old log like you can come back to life!—she commented. Adding—: I didn't think I'd ever lay eyes on you again, cockfighter.

—So what you up to, Bernarda? What you doing here, in this dump?

—I got here late and when I took a peek inside the arena the stage was already taken. What about you?

—Same old stuff.

—I was right when I said you'd been bitten by the bug... Invite me for a drink. Round here they wouldn't even offer you water if you were dying of thirst.

They headed for the cantina and ordered: for him, a red currant juice; for her, a pint of tequila.

—Yep, Bernarda, I had a hunch you'd be hanging around here in Cuquío. I was hoping to see you over by the roosters.

—I'm telling you these guys got here awful early. Mostly it was that bitchy Lucrecia Salcedo. Anyway, there's enough to go around, as long as no one gets pushy.

—Well, I've just come from Lorenzo Benavides's home. He didn't want to come along. Said this wasn't his type of place.

—No, it's not; he only goes to the big events.

—And by the way, Bernarda, what are you to Lorenzo Benavides?

—I'm not exactly his *mamá*, am I?

—Of course not.

They kept silent for a bit. A tear slid down her face, round and shiny like the eyes from which it sprang, as if it were one more glass bead like the others that she wore hanging around her neck.

—I didn't mean to offend you, Bernarda.

—Do I look offended? I'm just sad, which is something else—she said wiping away the tear with the back of her hand and another one that was just beginning to form.

—Did you love him?

—He's the one that was in love with me. But he tried to tie me down. To shut me up in his house. No one can do that to me... I just can't. What for? To waste my life away?

—Perhaps that could've been a good thing. His place is huge.

—Yea, but it has walls.

—And what's wrong with that?

She shrugged her shoulders as an explanation. She turned her attention toward the musicians and noticed that one of them was gesturing for her with his guitar, calling her up.

—Be right back—she told Dionisio Pinzón—. Wait for me.

She climbed onto the platform that served as her stage and after the mariachi band set about strumming their guitars she began her song:

Now the latches are all shut
for no one knows quite how to live;
and yet the hope I have not lost
that in your arms I still might lie:
Oh, how troubled is my luck,
that makes me so in love with you.
Once before you pledged your heart,
promised to not disdain my love;
I won't retire nor turn away
nor leave you for another one.
And even though bright pearls gleam
way out deep in the open sea;
there is still hope I have not lost
that in your arms some day I'll rest.

She left the stage wiping from her face the smile that she had offered the crowd in exchange for their applause. The roulette wheel began to spin amid the insistent calls of the croupiers until the shout of *¡Hecho el tiro!* announced that the ball was in play. That was followed by: Black four! and the sound of the jingling of pesos all up and down the table that was packed with customers.

La Caponera returned to Dionisio Pinzón's side. She took a swallow from her still nearly full glass and her body shook, perhaps from how weak the alcohol was.

—Nasty watered-down booze—she commented—. It's always the same in these places—she took the glass and threw its contents to the ground in a show of disgust. She seemed nervous, restless, maybe due to Dionisio Pinzón's questions. He stared at her intently, humbly, while she caressed her arms with hands that were covered in bracelets. As Dionisio gazed at *La Caponera* he had the feeling that she was way too attractive for him; as if she were one of those things that are too far out of one's reach to ever be an actual object of one's love. Thus, his gaze began to turn from one of simple observation to one of utter desire, as if that were the only thing within his reach: staring at and savoring her at will.

But that type of a look can penetrate and she felt it. She raised her eyes and for a moment held Dionisio Pinzón's stare. Quickly she dropped her gaze as if contemplating the empty glass.

She said:

—I need a drink! Let's go someplace where they don't rip you off.

But in response Dionisio called to the waiter:

—Bring me a closed bottle of *mezcal*!

And turning to *La Caponera*:

—It's gotta be the same everywhere. It's just business—he paused and later added—: From one hustler to another, that is. Don't you think?

She concurred with a smile.

The glass was filled once again, this time from the bottle that the server left on the table. Bernarda Cutiño gave it a try and then took a long and anxious drink. She seemed to return to life.

—When are you done here?—asked Dionisio Pinzón.

—At midnight.

—You can't imagine how much I'd love for you to go with me to the cockfights. You're my good luck charm.

—A lot of guys have already told me that. Lorenzo Benavides

among them. I must be good for something, since whoever I'm with can't seem to lose.

—I'll bet. I've seen it myself.

—Yep. Everyone has used me. But then...

She took another drink of *mezcal*, while listening to Dionisio say:

—I'll never abandon you, Bernanda.

—I know—she responded.

She finished what was left in her glass, grabbed the bottle and, while getting to her feet and motioning toward the musicians, announced:

—I'm gonna take this to my *muchachos*. See you in a bit.

He watched as she headed off in the direction of the stage where the mariachis waited for her.

A bit later, Dionisio Pinzón was back at the pen where he had secured his roosters. He untied one of them from the stake and caressed its belly. He inspected its wings and legs and sprayed a mouthful of water on its head since it was so hot that the animal was hissing as if it couldn't breathe. He took it in his arms and, all the while stroking its back, wandered around the enclosure gesturing and speaking to himself, repeating over and over again a portion of his conversation with Bernarda.

He walked around like that for quite awhile. That is until he turned around and saw the worker whose job it was to care for the roosters staring at him curiously. So he grabbed his animal with both hands and bounded toward the arena.

From that moment on Dionisio Pinzón and Bernarda Cutiño wandered the land going from festival to festival, alternating between the cockfights, the roulette wheel, and card games. It was as if his joining up with *La Caponera* had assured his luck and lifted his spirits, and he always seemed confident at any game, as if he knew the outcome before it happened.

He had discovered, and now he was confirming, that by her side it was difficult for him to lose, which made him impulsive often to the point of risking more than he could pay back, tempting a fate that always favored him.

He married *La Caponera* on some day and in some town just like any other, making good on his promise to never leave her side.

She wasn't really interested in marriage. But something deep down was telling her that this guy was not like all the others and, motivated by the benefits of forming an alliance with someone, especially with someone like Dionisio Pinzón who was full of greed and who she was sure was the type who, like her, would just keep bouncing around while they plucked the feathers off the very last of their birds, she agreed to wed, since at least that way she'd have someone to accompany her in her solitary life.

They wandered among all the towns, cities, and farming villages. She because she loved it. He motivated by ambition and a boundless urge to accumulate wealth.

ONE DAY, SOME TIME LATER, Dionisio Pinzón decided to visit his old friend Lorenzo Benavides who had abandoned the festival circuit and whom he hadn't seen in forever.

They arrived one afternoon at Santa Gertrudis, by then accompanied by their daughter, a young girl now ten years old. They found Benavides planted in a wheelchair, old and worn out. Despite it all, he was thrilled to see them. He kissed both of Bernarda Cutiño's hands and caressed the daughter as if she were his own. He hadn't lost his old personality and was still vain and overbearing.

—I know you've done well—he told Dionisio Pinzón—. And I'm happy to see you both. I hope you don't get bored with my bad company for however many days your visit lasts.

—We're leaving right away—*La Caponera* responded—. We're just passing through and only stopped to say hello.

—That's right, Don Lorenzo—Pinzón added—. We owed you this visit and many more, but you understand how busy one gets when the whole world is your home... It's just that you shouldn't take our absence as ingratitude...

—What you need is to settle down... Relax a bit. After all, a tree that doesn't take root can't grow... As for a place to stay, I can offer you my house now and whenever.

—Much obliged, Don Lorenzo.

—And to change the subject, how's your game of *Paco*? I'm guessing you've forgotten it all.

—I haven't forgotten anything I learned from you.

—So stay 'til tomorrow! It'll be good fun to play a little hand tonight.

AND THEY STAYED.

The pair sat around a marble-covered table dealing cards to keep the game going. Not far away, seated in the same high-backed chair that she had occupied since arriving, Bernarda Cutiño looked on with her daughter asleep on her lap. Lorenzo Benavides explained:

—I'm not up to playing with cash since I've got so little of that left; but I've got a *ranchito* close by. It's your call.

—A rancho? And how much is it worth to you?

—Good. I'll let you know what you owe me when you've lost. You in?

—I'm in, Don Lorenzo, ain't got no reason to complain.

THEY PLAYED.

—You lose, Don Lorenzo. What else can you put up?

—This house—he said—. Against the rancho and... let's say fifty thousand pesos. Don't you think it's worth that?

—Whatever you say. After all, we're just messing around.

—No, Pinzón. This is for real. I know you can't beat me.

—Let's get at it, then.

—Cut!—Lorenzo Benavides ordered after shuffling the deck.

Dionisio Pinzón divided the cards into different piles on the table. Benavides picked one up and asked:

—Does this work?

—Yep.

Benavides announced the cards as if they weren't obvious:

—Six of Swords and Page of Cups.

Dionisio Pinzón, recalling that the Page was a particularly bad card for him, selected the Six of Swords.

—Another card, or are you done?

—I'm in.

When the tenth card was dealt the Six appeared. One solitary Six of Coins.

—The house is yours—Lorenzo Benavides said dryly.

—I'll give you one more shot, Don Lorenzo...You choose the card.

—A rematch with what wager? Myself?—he said pushing away from the table and showing his impairment—...Tell me, could you match this?

—I'm not gonna take your house. You know that... I figured we were just playing for the fun of it... Besides, I've gotta admit I owe everything I have to you.

For the fun of it? If you would've lost you'd see what kind of fun I'd make of you... No, Pinzón. Not even my own father would ever forgive one of my gambling debts...And what you say about owing me for everything you are, you're wrong. Look here...

He wheeled his chair over to Bernarda Cutiño, who looked at him perplexed and drew a smile on her lips. But without warning, an angry Lorenzo Benavides startled her with a tremendous slap that put an end to her expression, all the while screaming in her face:

—...You owe everything to this filthy *bruja*!

And then, with eyes still injected with hatred and with an irritated expression carved on his face, he headed off into the darkness of the hall, pushing hard to speed up the invalid's chair in which he sat.

Dionisio Pinzón, without getting worked up, shuffled and re-shuffled the cards that had been abandoned...

TIME LET ITS YEARS PASS BY. In the same mansion of Santa Gertrudis and in the exact same spot, Dionisio Pinzón, as if he hadn't changed his posture from so many years earlier, continued shuffling. Facing him and sitting around a table covered in green cloth was a gathering of *señores* waiting to receive their cards. They were playing *Paco Grande*. The eight decks were shuffled together, cut, and cut again until the dealing began.

A bit behind Dionisio sat *La Caponera*, as if she too hadn't moved from her position. Sitting in the same armchair, half hidden in the shadows of the large room, she seemed more symbol than living being. But it was her. And it was her duty to always be there. And even though instead of colored beads she now sported a pearl necklace that stood out against the black backdrop of her dress and her hands were spiked with diamonds, she was not content. She had never been content.

There were frequent disputes with her husband. Bitter and resentful arguments in which she blamed him for the captivity in which he forced her to live.

At first, and because of the birth of her daughter, she had accepted this confinement voluntarily; but when her little one began to grow, becoming a girl and then a woman, her desire to be free clashed with the intransigence of her husband who had enjoyed having a stable place to live.

She, on the other hand, was accustomed to freedom and to the open spaces of the fairs and felt crushed in the desolation of that immense house, languishing from so much lassitude. Night after night, Dionisio Pinzón forced her to stay in the corner of the great hall within sight of the card players, cut off from the sun and the light of day since the games would end at the crack of dawn and begin at sunset. That's how her days grew dark and, instead of breathing in the air of new environments, she sucked down the smoke and alcohol-laced breath that permeated in this one.

La Caponera had once been able to set the conditions and to impose her own will, but that was before Dionisio Pinzón had abandoned his humble disposition for one of arrogance. But now, with her voice in decline and her strength gone, she was left with no other option than to obey someone else's whim and to deny her own existence.

—Listen to me good, Dionisio—she had demanded when he asked her to marry him—, I'm not used to being bossed around. That's why I chose this life… And I'm the one that gets to decide who I want to be with and who I want to get rid of, whenever I want. You're no better and no worse than anyone else. I'm warning you now.

—That's fine, Bernarda, you can have it your way.

—It's not that. What I need is a man. Not for his protection since I know how to take care of myself; but I do want him to be able to stand up for me and for himself… And he can't panic if I make his life a living hell.

But as it turned out, he was the one that made her life miserable. He was never the same after he got a taste for the power that money bought him. He became smug and set out to prove himself better than everyone else. And even when Bernarda fought back with whatever she had at hand to not lose her independent way of life, her efforts always proved ineffective and she would have to give in. But she did resist. That's why when Dionisio Pinzón tried to settle at Santa Gertrudis, the mansion that he had won at cards from Lorenzo Benavides, she didn't wake up at his side the next morning. She disappeared, taking her daughter along. He, believing this to be little more than a passing fancy, waited at Santa Gertrudis for her return, calculating that she couldn't get too far without money and with the girl in tow. He must have forgotten that he was dealing with *La Caponera*, a tough woman full of determination.

On the other hand, there's probably no need to point out that this became a dark time for Pinzón as his luck faded, so much so that it wasn't just that damned game of *Paco* that cut into his fortune. His roosters, managed independently but competently by Secundino Colmenero, were also disappearing one by one, erased by a cruel fate.

Secundino Colmenero showed up at Santa Gertrudis after a number of excursions to various arenas only to report that two dozen of his best animals had been killed, even in events known for the poor quality of the chickens that fought there. What's worse, the only birds left in their pen were all "throwaways," gamecocks that were already old and burned-out, used only to warm up the others for combat. And, if that weren't enough, all of his money was gone, seeing as he had bet like crazy on matches that he was sure he would win. He simply couldn't understand what was going on, since, as he explained it, no one but himself had fed, tied up, or fought the animals; although, as he concluded, you can't do anything against bad luck.

Dionisio Pinzón didn't blame Colmenero for the losses, just like he couldn't blame himself either. He asked about Bernarda. And Secundino responded that yes he had seen her. The last time in a place called Árbol Grande, not that far away.

And that wasn't all, adding that he had spoken with her each time the two had crossed paths. No, he hadn't seen any indication that she was unhappy. Just that she no longer sang with the women who performed at the cockfights now that her voice was beginning to grow tired and could no longer be heard in the open spaces of the arenas. These days she and her musicians were setting up in cantinas and *canela* bars. But no, she hadn't seemed sad at all. And once she had even told him, among other things, that if it weren't for his daughter she wouldn't remember Dionisio Pinzón at all.

Convinced that without Bernarda he would never be able to regain his loses and much less build the fortune that he so wanted, Dionisio Pinzón swallowed his pride and headed out to search for her. Árbol Grande was not far and he arrived early the next day. He inquired in all of the stalls and cantinas, until finally he heard the words of a particular tune and saw a crowd gathered around the entrance of an establishment that led him straight to where she was. At her side, dressed exactly like her mother, was their daughter.

Dionisio waited for Bernarda to finish the song and for everyone to clear out of the confined space before he approached. And that's where they spoke.

—You know good and well I was born to be out and about. And that I'll only settle down the day they throw dirt down on my dead body.

—I just imagined that now that you have a daughter that you'd want to give her a different life.

—Just the opposite, I want her to follow in my footsteps so she doesn't have to answer to anybody... You don't know me at all,

Dionisio Pinzón! And I'm telling you right now that as long as I'm strong enough to get around I won't be walled in.

—Is that your final word?

—It always has been.

—That's fine, Bernarda, we can stay together under those conditions. I'll do my best to get you back singing in the cockfights.

—No, Dionisio. They don't want me there. They need a strong voice, and mine is starting to break.

—Soon they won't take you anywhere.

—Is that what you think?

—Yep. I'm sure of it. *¡Vamos!*

And that's how Dionisio Pinzón returned to a pilgrim's life of wandering from town to town accompanied by *La Caponera*. She, getting in a few songs here and there, followed by the members of her mariachi band. He, bouncing back and forth between the cockfights and the card games and between the card games and the cockfights, all in an effort to regain his lost winnings. Every now and then they would stop in at Santa Gertrudis, but they would never stay more than one or two weeks before heading back on the road.

UNTIL THE DAY SHE DREADED ARRIVED. The guys from the mariachi band left her. Business wasn't going well. *La Caponera* drank a lot and her voice was worn out, nearly hoarse, and few people were eager to listen to her anymore. So the musicians looked for another singer and didn't want anything more to do with Bernarda Cutiño.

Nor was she able to attract other musicians by showing them that her daughter was also good at singing. Wasn't that why she had toughened her up, so that when she began to fade there would be someone who could take her place? Yet everyone complained that the girl was still too young and that even though she was pretty good they would end up having to drag the mother along and take care of her as well.

—No, business just ain't good enough to support both a singer and her mother—they declared.

That's when Dionisio Pinzón laid out his own terms. First of all, they locked themselves up in the mansion at Santa Gertrudis. He had money again and converted the house into a gathering place for hardcore players of the games of *Malilla*, *Siete y Medio*, and *Paco Grande*. Night after night the house stayed awake, with its lights burning, playing witness to groups of silent men who, gathered around their tables, were caught up in their cards.

Don Dionisio, as he was now called, provided everything for his guests, the best wines and the best food, so that no one had any reason to leave Santa Gertrudis for several days, with many taking advantage of that convenience.

But the person who most benefited from the situation was himself. Tired of having to travel the world in pursuit of wealth, here it would simply fall into his open hands without him ever having to go out and search for it. Furthermore, his luck was boundless and he soon owned several properties that were won through the tricks of the game but that he had no desire to manage, accepting whatever his tenants freely sent his way, which was quite a bit. Even with all that, he had not forgotten about, nor ignored, his impressive collection of gamecocks, still in the care of Secundino Colmenero. Every now and then he would organize or attend a fight, although he dedicated most of his time to playing cards where, according to him, he always won more and did so more quickly. *La Caponera* had become a submissive and exhausted woman. Now lacking her previous strength, she not only gave in to holing up in that house as if she were a prisoner but, with his wife truly transformed into his good luck charm, Dionisio Pinzón determined that she should always be there with the gamblers in the great hall, close to him or at least where he could sense her presence.

At first she would attend the gatherings on her own, wanting to be a part of the company of others and not feel so isolated. But she soon discovered that there was nothing pleasant about gazing upon those men in their long and tiresome games and she decided not to return. But Pinzón ordered her quite forcefully back to the place where she was expected to fulfill her role. Without any concern for whether his wife, completely alone and without any one to speak to, slept or stayed awake, whether she dwelled on the past or cursed her present condition.

This all came about one morning when Dionisio Pinzón systematically began to lose what he had won during the course of the night and even a bit more. He complained that he was feeling tired and blamed his inability to concentrate on the game to his long hours without sleep. His companions gave him a moment of rest and noticed, when he returned to continue the match, that with him, hidden in the shadows, sat Bernarda Cutiño.

No one seemed to think this out of the ordinary, since they were quite accustomed to seeing her there. And as she tended to remain so still, as if she were sleeping, those in attendance, absorbed in the game, quickly forgot about the woman and worried only about their own circumstances, especially as they began to notice how the pile of winnings was passing once again into the hands of Dionisio Pinzón, who was accumulating huge amounts of money.

From that time on, until the night of her passing, this was the life that Bernarda Cutiño led. She gave the appearance of being a permanent shadow settled in a high-backed armchair; after all, it was difficult to make out her face or to gauge her movements, seeing as she always wore black and hid from the light that illuminated little more than the circle of card players. She, on the other hand, could well observe all of the others from her obscurity.

Dionisio Pinzón was hardly concerned that *La Caponera*, in an attempt to fill those long and sleepless nights, would drink until she passed out from bottles that she kept close at hand. Because that's exactly what she was doing from the spot where her husband had planted her. And that's why she would seem to be a bit restless at first before becoming motionless.

What's certain is that she was well accustomed to drinking. Ever since she got her start as a singer at the cockfights it had been expected that she would wet her whistle between songs with a long drink of tequila that some spectator, a triumphant gambler, or a love-struck fan would offer her and her musicians and that would help them add a bit more life and feeling to their performance. After that she never lost the habit of drinking alcohol.

It's hardly unexpected then that here in her own home, where she did absolutely nothing, not even singing, since even that pleasure had been taken from her, that she would fill her long hours with alcohol and then sleep off her drunkenness in front of unspeaking gamblers who sat around a table playing *Paco* during long and soundless nights where even the tedious dealing of the cards could barely be heard. It was thus in the presence of these few silent men who seemed even to mask the sound of their own breathing that she would drink and drink until she would finally fall sound asleep, soothed by her intoxicated and beating heart.

But she wasn't making a mess just of her own life; she had also neglected that of her child, about whom she no longer seemed to know anything. And Dionisio Pinzón was no different, not thinking at all about the daughter that was also called Bernarda and nicknamed *La Pinzona*, all because his heart was set so firmly on his gambling.

For her part, the young woman never sought her parents out for anything. She came and went as she pleased. She would disappear for a few days. And then come back. She would disappear again, without ever seeing them, nor they her.

One morning, after another crippling night without sleep the two were headed up to their bedrooms to rest, he up front with *La Caponera* stumbling behind, when a few individuals arrived from the nearby village claiming to be community representatives and wanting to speak with Dionisio Pinzón.

They laid out the reason for their visit, indicating that they had come on account of the younger Bernarda:

—*Señor*—they said—, perhaps because of the demands on your time you are unaware of the conduct of your daughter.

And Dionisio Pinzón, who was easily agitated, especially at times like these when he was overcome with fatigue, responded:

—Why the hell would you be interested in the conduct of my

daughter?

Just at that moment, staggering and looking to hold herself up against a wall, Bernarda Cutiño approached:

—What do these *señores* want, Dionisio? What are they saying?... Has something happened to Bernardita?

But Dionisio Pinzón, without paying any attention to his wife, again confronted the group of *señores*:

—I want to know: what gives you the right to stick your noses where they don't belong?

One of them finally spoke up, timidly:

—We thought maybe... she was taking advantage of your benevolence, Don Dionisio... We felt it was our responsibility to make you aware of her licentious activities... Her scandalous lack of restraint, even within the sanctity of the homes of our town... Just yesterday...

What about yesterday?—shouted Dionisio Pinzón—! I don't want to hear your gossip!

—I must tell you, Don Dionisio—intervened one of the gentlemen—; my daughter Sofía was supposed to get married today. We had everything ready... The church... the banquet... everything. And precisely yesterday, her fiancé, Trinidad Arias, was abducted by that daughter of yours...

—And she abused one of my boys, named Alfonso, only seventeen years old, just two weeks ago...—declared another person who was present.

—It's not just that, *señor* Don Dionisio—remarked a guy with a waxed moustache—. I am, as you can see, a respectable man. Respectful of the home where I have produced six children. Two of them, regrettably, died young... Today they are resting in the arms of the Lord... And even I, if you can imagine, have received amorous advances from *La Pinzona*; in other words, from your daughter... at the risk of...

—The point is—added another in a haughty voice while gesticulating wildly— that an alliance of *señoras*, mothers, and wives see their homes placed in danger with the shamelessly coquettish behavior of that girl... And her indecent provocations.

And with the cat finally out of the bag, they all simmered with their various accusations against Bernarda Pinzón.

A troubled Bernarda Cutiño listened to everything that was being said about her daughter while her eyes passed anxiously over all of those *señores* who were demanding, like an outcry, a severe punishment for the child that she had brought into the world and that, without her knowing exactly when, had grown up and started down the same path that had been her own life.

Dionisio Pinzón, on the other hand, accustomed to having everyone defer to his power and fortune, and feeling a sense of pride in the conduct of his daughter, looked on those *señores* with contempt and scorn. He let them say their piece and then yelled angrily:

—Get out of here! *Imbéciles!* Filthy scum!—And in a chorus of additional insults, he threw them out of his house.

He returned to Bernarda Cutiño's side, who blurted out while sobbing: It can't be true!, still unable to believe what had been said about her daughter. Dionisio took her by the shoulders and pulled her away from the wall where she had rested her head. And he explained to her in words still filled with ire:

—My daughter will do whatever the hell she wants! You hear

me, Bernarda? And while I'm alive I'll make sure she gets whatever she fancies, no matter who gets hurt.

Having calmed a bit, he had his wife lean against him and helped her toward her room while explaining:

—Don't worry, Bernarda... She'll settle down some day... Just like you did. Just like we all do... Go and get some rest.

But Bernarda would never be comforted again. She felt guilty and tormented by her daughter's future. Which served to make her existence even more unpleasant. And she went on drinking and getting drunk to the point of insanity.

One night she passed away all alone, seated in the same chair as always, without anyone coming to her aid or being aware of the alcohol-induced asphyxia that led to her death.

It was raining on that night, as it had been without interruption for the space of many nights, giving the card players a welcome excuse to extend their stay at Santa Gertrudis. Those in attendance were all men of means, including a retired general, the owner of a nearby hacienda; two brothers named Arriaga, natives of San Luis Potosí and claiming to be lawyers, but who were actually nothing more than professional gamblers; a wealthy miner from Pinos; and a ranch owner from the Bajío accompanied by his doctor, since he seemed to have a bad heart, which didn't keep him from being the only player who downed glass after glass of *aguardiente*, mixing them every now and then with various flasks of medicine that he kept at hand, right there on the table. He drew attention to himself because he was always taking something "for his nerves" or "for the fun of it," depending on whether he was winning or losing. The doctor, for his part, would check his patient's pulse every now and then, or take a stethoscope to his heart, although this never kept the guy from participating in the game.

All in all there were seven individuals sitting around the table that night. The same ones that had already played for several nights without showing any sign of fatigue.

As always, the gathering had begun after dinner. Except for the sound made by the rain falling outside, everything was absolutely quiet, and one might assume that the great hall was unoccupied if not for the muted sound of some movement occasionally made by one of those figures, a cough to clear a throat, or, at the end of each hand, when the eight decks were returned to the center of the table in an impressive pile, or some brief comment or joke that Dionisio Pinzón allowed himself to make at the expense of one of his guests.

The pile of money belonged to the rancher from the Bajío. But it didn't last long in his hands. It was quickly passing, between the pills and the drinks, to the general's control. And from there on to Dionisio, where it didn't move for the space of several hours. It continued to accumulate until four of the attendees withdrew from the game, leaving only the two lawyers from San Luis facing off against Dionisio Pinzón.

To one side, in the shadows where she always hid, Bernarda Cutiño rested, motionless, seeming to be asleep. Her figure, barely touched by the reflection of the light, stood out in the penumbra because of the dark black that she wore since, like on so many other occasions, she donned a dress made of black velvet that was accompanied by her ever-present pearl necklace and a brilliant diamond on one of her hands.

The rain stopped very close to the break of dawn, which was announced by the crowing of the cocks and the frogs croaking in the soggy fields.

Of those men who had abandoned the game the only one who was still in attendance was the guy with the bad heart, with his doctor still at his side, both fast asleep with their heads resting on the back of their chairs. The others had begun the trip back to their own homes.

Dionisio Pinzón continued to play with his usual relaxed demeanor, even though the two Arriaga brothers had conspired to defeat him. His face, tense from trying to stay calm, showed neither fear nor jubilation. It appeared to be made of stone.

Finally, one of the brothers threw down his cards to indicate that he was done. And he left.

Pinzón calculated that the other would follow in the next hand and that once again he had the game won; and that's why he didn't bother to protest when he saw the so-called lawyer, his only opponent, pull a fast one while dealing the cards. What's more, he even let him win the point.

—It's yours *licenciado*—he said, even before seeing his hand. But he stared him down as if to say: you're a bit ham-fisted to be cheating. The rival seemed to understand, gave the cards to Dionisio Pinzón, and said:

—You shuffle and deal.

And that's what happened.

Suddenly Dionisio felt that he was losing. He saw how his winnings were eroding.

—Just carelessness—he said in his defense.

But an hour later he had been cleaned out and his entire pile now belonged to the lawyer from San Luis.

That's when he heard a girl's laugh. It was a sonorous and cheerful chuckle that seemed to want to pierce the night.

He turned his head toward the spot where his wife was resting; but she seemed at peace, sound asleep and untroubled by the laugh that had him so bothered.

—That's gotta be my daughter. She tends to get home about this hour—he said as if he were responding to some question.

And yet it seemed that neither of the two Arriaga brothers had asked anything. The one that was still in the game looked him full on:

—Your call, Don Dionisio—he told him.

He looked at his cards and threw them down on the green cloth:

—I'm out—he responded.

From some corner of the house came the sound of a far off voice that began to sing:

> Go and ask the distant stars
> if at night they see me cry;
> ask them if I will not find
> the solitude that love demands.
> Go and ask the gentle river
> if it feels my flowing tears;
> go and ask the world wide
> if my sorrow is not deep...

And, as if in reply, he heard the same song in the passionate voice of *La Caponera*, over there, coming from the stage of some cockfighting arena, while he looked down at a shiny golden rooster that was rolling around on the ground, dead.

He heard the voice again:

—You deal, Don Dionisio.

As if distracted, he picked up the cards from his previous hand. He looked at them again and repeated:

—I'm out.

—If you're tired, we can leave this for another time—said the guy sitting in front of him.

—No, no way—he responded, coming back to his senses—… Not on your life. Let's go.

—You have anything to play?

—What's that?

The cocks crowed again, perhaps finally announcing the arrival of the sun. The beating of their wings gave off a hollow echo and they sang, one after another, without end.

His mother was there helping him make a hole in the ground, while he, squatting, tried to bring a bloodied and half-dead game-cock back to life by blowing into its beak.

He shook his head to scare away his thoughts.

—What?—he asked again.

—If you have anything to throw in—, was the answer.

—Yea, of course. In that safe over there—he said pointing to a vault built into the wall— I've got a bit of money. Plenty to cover the pot and… a bit more.

—Good enough. It can cover the pot then.

—Let's go.

He lost again.

He held in his hands for just a moment the worthless cards that luck had played to him and, out of the corner of his eyes, he glanced over at his wife who continued to sleep, not at all restless.

—Want to keep playing, Don Dionisio?

—Of course.

—You want to pay up now or later?

He headed over to the safe and returned with all of its contents, from cash money to papers that represented the deeds to his properties. He paid off what he had lost. He took the cards, shuffled, and then dealt. While doing so he noticed that he didn't feel at all fatigued, although perhaps a bit uneasy due to the unsettling thoughts that kept him distracted.

The cards fell and kept on falling, hastening the misfortune of Dionisio Pinzón, who became unnerved and lost his composure. A cold sweat of despair began pouring down his face. He was now playing blindly, without winning. He played again and lost again. He didn't want to leave the deck unattended for even a moment and placed it under his elbow as soon as he dealt the cards.

—I can't lose—he kept saying—. I can't lose—while mumbling other incoherencies.

The rancher from the Bajío and his doctor, now both awake, as well as the other lawyer who was now just a bystander, observed it all without flinching, not believing their eyes or understanding the blunders that this guy was committing, who just moments earlier had been so calm, so in control of himself, yet was now losing hand over fist everything he seemed to own on this earth.

—You're risking your future, Don Dionisio. There's no reason for you to play this way— the rancher dared to say.

But Pinzón didn't listen.

Morning had already broken. The light that came in through the enormous windows flooded the green cloth that covered the table, illuminating the faces of the players, exhausted from a lack of sleep. Dionisio Pinzón was now wagering his last document. He placed his cards face down, while the other guy examined his own hand. When two more cards were requested Dionisio dealt them out and continued to wait. He looked in the direction of Bernarda Cutiño, her face pale, peacefully asleep. Then he looked toward his adversary, attempting to divine any sign, any trace of discouragement. Only then did he reach for his cards. His hands were shaking and his eyes gave off a metallic shine. He threw down three and picked up three others, but he didn't even arrange them. His competitor showed him his hand, and Dionisio had nothing to beat it. Not even two of a kind.

—Bernarda!—he called out—. Bernarda! Wake up, Bernarda! We've lost it all! You hear me?

He headed over to his wife. He shook her by the shoulders:

—You hear me, Bernarda? We've lost everything! Even this!

And with one strong pull he ripped the pearl necklace that Bernarda Cutiño had around her neck, sending the beads scattering across the floor.

—He kept screaming: Wake up Bernarda!

The doctor who had stuck around approached the pair. He pushed Dionisio Pinzón aside and, raising the woman's eyelids with his fingers while listening to her heart with a stethoscope, he said:

—She's not going to wake up... She's dead.

With that Dionisio's miscalculation became abundantly clear

as he kept shaking his wife and yelling at her:

—Why didn't you let me know you had died, Bernarda?

His daughter, Bernarda *La Pinzona*, came to investigate all of the shouting. And only upon seeing her did Dionisio Pinzón seem to relax.

—Come and say goodbye to your mother—he told the girl.

She, understanding what had happened, ran forward and threw herself at her dead mother.

Meanwhile, Dionisio turned to face the guy who that night had won all that he had.

—In that room I've been keeping a casket—he said pointing toward a small door at the side of the great hall—. That wasn't part of the wager... Everything, but not the casket.

He immediately left the room. His footsteps could be heard for a short while as he walked the length of the mansion's long corridor. Soon after came the sound of a single gunshot, as if someone had slapped a cowhide with a rod.

THEY BURIED THEM THAT SAME AFTERNOON in the small cemetery at Santa Gertrudis. She in a black box, made in a rush and with cheap wood. He in the gray casket with silver molding that he had kept hidden since that time when he was unable to use it to hold his mother's remains.

Only two individuals accompanied the bodies to the graveyard. Secundino Colmenero and Bernarda Pinzón. Not one of the many guests that had stayed so often at Santa Gertrudis showed up, and those who had been there cleared out without taking their leave, as if they were afraid of becoming accomplices in that double passing. Even the gravediggers, after finishing their handiwork, disappeared in different directions.

When the two were alone, facing the twin crosses they had driven over the same grave, Secundino Colmenero asked:

—What's gonna become of you now, Bernarda?

She, wearing a sad face, contrite, as if she bore not only the weight of those two deaths, but also that of her own guilt, shrugged her shoulders and, in a voice that was full of bitterness, said:

—There's no way I could live here... I'll follow my mother's destiny. That's how I can honor her wishes.

A FEW DAYS LATER, that girl who had come to have it all and now had nothing to support her in life except her voice was singing from the stage of a cockfighting ring in Cocotlán, a town hidden away in one of the most isolated corners of Mexico. There she performed just as her mother had done in her earliest moments, singing songs bursting with her own sense of abandonment.

> *Beautiful peacock my messenger be*
> *as you travel along distant roads,*
> *if someone happens to ask 'bout me,*
> *beautiful peacock tell 'em I cry,*
> *honest tears straight from the heart*
> *for a true woman that I hold dear...*

—Close the doors!—shouted the announcer to start the fights.

SYNOPSIS OF THE GOLDEN COCKEREL[18]

The Golden Cockerel tells the story of a poverty-stricken man, Dionisio Pinzón, who is unable to work on account of a mutilated arm, which is why he plies the trade of "town crier" in a remote Mexican village. Since he was also employed to "announce" the cockfights, one day someone gives him a half-dead rooster. With the help of his mother, an old and sickly woman, Pinzón buries the bird in a hole, leaving only the head above ground. Eventually, his efforts to save the cockerel succeed, and yet, in the very moment that his animal comes around, his mother passes away. Without enough money to buy a coffin, Pinzón pries some rotting boards from the door of his house, making something a bit like a cage that he lugs on his shoulders to the cemetery. The town's inhabitants, supposing he's off to bury some dead animal, make fun of Pinzón, who decides to abandon the village forever, accompanied by his golden cockerel.

That's how he ends up on the open road, passing through

---

18   The typewritten original of this synopsis was found among the author's personal papers and published, for the first time, in 2010 (*El gallo de oro*. By Juan Rulfo. Mexico City: Editorial RM and Fundación Juan Rulfo, pp. 75–78). Dated January 8, 1959, the text was almost certainly composed by Rulfo as an introduction to his storyline as it was being considered for adaptation to film. A few details that diverge from the novel add to the piece's interest and importance.

numerous towns and battling his rooster in local fairs where cock-fights are held. He travels from San Juan del Río all the way to Chavinda, and from there he shows up in Aguascalientes and later in Rincón de Romos, winning matches in all of these places. In Aguascalientes he meets a "singer," nicknamed *La Caponera*, on account of the sway she holds over men. She's a tall and gritty woman who sings with a lot of heart from one cockfight to the next, and who knows how to spurn or to love whomever she pleases. At the end of the festivities, Pinzón collects his bird and runs into a fellow named Colmenero, with *La Caponera*, who seems to be his lover, tagging along. He's a typical guy from the highlands, all decked out in leather and formidable in his appearance. They sit down to quench their thirst at one of those make-shift stalls that are routinely erected at these fairs. With Pinzón seated right next to them, Colmenero looks him straight in the eye and, with a condescending voice, offers to buy the golden cock-erel. Pinzón responds that it's not for sale. The highlander, overly confident in his wealth, insists over and over again until he finally sees the futility of his approach and, with *La Caponera* throwing in her own words of support, he suggests an arrangement that only the most experienced cockers know about. All the same, Pinzón turns them down since he has no intention of playing dirty with an animal in which he has so much confidence. In the end, the golden cockerel is killed in Tlaquepaque, fighting against a bird owned by Colmenero. Pinzón loses everything he's won to that point. He tries to earn something back at the card tables, but loses again. From there he hears the commotion of the cockpit. As he gets up to leave, he feels the hand of *La Caponera* on his shoulder.

The woman gives him a bundle of pesos wrapped in a scarf and compels him to continue betting. This time he wins. And both of them return to the cockfights. He accepts the deal that Colmenero had previously offered and joins forces with him in the difficult art of fighting cocks.

From that moment on, Pinzón and *La Caponera* will travel the world together. Eventually, she leaves the other guy and agrees to marry Pinzón, convinced that his ambition might facilitate her fondness for traveling from festival to festival. In time, and now with a daughter between them, the couple visits Colmenero at his ranch in San Juan Sin Agua. They find him a bit discouraged, seated in a wheelchair. At his urging, they play *Paco Grande* and Colmenero loses the ranch and a few other properties. Pinzón decides to stay and live at the house, going against his wife's preference. In time, she decides to head out on her own. But with her voice starting to wear out, she's forced to go back. Pinzón lays out a few conditions. He's converted the ranch into a gambling house and her job will be to remain by his side while the games are underway. Experience had taught him that his luck just wasn't the same without Bernarda Cutiño, *La Caponera*, since his fortune had withered during her absence.

That's why, whenever guests came to gamble, *La Caponera* could be found sitting in the dark recesses of the room, whether asleep or awake, until boredom led her to overdrink, something that she had done frequently during her time as a singer at the cockfights. That didn't bother Pinzón, as long as he had her close at hand, as if she were some sort of amulet. These days, she had taken to dressing all in black and would wear a pearl necklace that shined even in the shadows where she hid her face that was weary from intoxication. They paid little or no attention to their daughter. He, obsessed with gambling, she, shrouded in the fog of her alcohol. What's certain is that, for many, the young woman had become the terror of the town. She defiled young men, stole away husbands, and destroyed homes that earlier had seemed so close-knit that nothing would be able to break them apart. Her parents had no knowledge of their daughter's activities, nor at what time she was leaving home or getting back. And Pinzón wasn't going to let anyone keep his daughter from doing whatever she wanted, even in the face of protests from those representing the polite society of San Juan Sin Agua.

Then, on a night in which he had been winning large amounts of money at cards, Pinzón all of a sudden noticed that his pile was beginning to shrink. He attributed the bad luck to his own inattention; but the losses kept coming one after another, and by the time he lost property deeds and other important papers he got up from the table furious and went straight over to his wife to wake her and tell her what had happened. He shook her by the shoulders and tore off the pearl necklace that she had around her neck. A doctor who happened to be there attending to one of the participants with a bad heart, approached Bernarda Cutiño and calmly explained to Pinzón that the woman had died an hour earlier.

Pinzón went to the back of the house and put a bullet through his head. The next day the two of them were buried in the same grave.

Now we get a glimpse of the daughter as she follows in her

mother's footsteps, standing on the stage of some cockfighting arena where she blurts out the very songs that *La Caponera* had used to liven up those events.

Juan Rulfo

BEYOND THE PLAIN IN FLAMES:
A SAMPLING OF OTHER WRITINGS

THE SECRET FORMULA

I

You will say that it is pure nonsense my idea,
    that it is wrong-headed to complain about fate,
    and even more so about this harsh land
    where destiny forgot about us.

The truth is that it's difficult
    to get used to hunger.

And although they say that hunger
    when divided among many
    affects fewer,
    the only true thing is that here
    each one of us
    is half dead
    and we don't even have
    a place to lie down and die.

As it seems now
    things are going from bad to worse
None of this idea that we should turn a blind eye to

this matter.

None of that.

Since the beginning of time
  we have set out with our stomachs stuck to our ribs
    while hanging on by our fingernails against the wind.

People haggle with us even over our shadows,
  and despite it all
    here we are:
    half dazed by the cursed sun
    that beats us down every day
    always with the same syringe
    as if it wanted to stir up its hot ashes.
Even though we know all too well
  that not even burning on live coals
    will our luck catch fire.

But we are stubborn.

Perhaps there's some hope in all this.

The world is full of people like us,
  of many people like us.
And someone has to hear us,
    someone and some others,
      even though our cries
        annoy or upset them.

It's not that we are rebellious,
    nor is it that we are asking for the world.
Nor is it our tendency to look quickly for a refuge,
    or to head for the hills
every time some dogs bark at us.

Someone will have to hear us.

When we stop grumbling like wasps in
    a swarm,
        or when we become the funnel of a whirlwind,
        or when we end up fleeing over
        the land
        like a lightening flash of the dead,
        then
        perhaps
        a remedy
        will come to us all.

II

Lightening strike,
    whirlpool of the dead.
With the burden that they carry,
    little will their efforts last.
Perhaps they will end up shattered in the surf
    or swallowed by this air full of ashes.
And they can even lose themselves

groping along
in the muddy darkness.
After all, they are nothing but debris.

Their souls must have broken apart
from so much struggling to survive.
It could be that they suffer cramps among
the frozen threads of the night,
or that fear will destroy them
erasing even their breath.

Saint Matthew has been seen since yesterday
with his face darkened.
Pray for us.

Blessed souls in purgatory.
Pray for us.

So high is the night and unable to watch over them.
Pray for us.

Holy God, Holy Immortal.
Pray for us.

Already everyone is a bit feeble from how much the sun
has sapped their energy.
Pray for us.

Holy Saint Anthony.

Pray for us.

Bunch of villains, gathering of bums.

Pray for us.

Cluster of vagrants, stream of idlers.

Pray for us.

Flock of bandits.

Pray for us.

At least these ones will no longer live overwhelmed by hunger.

LIFE DOESN'T TAKE ITSELF VERY SERIOUSLY

The cradle where Crispín used to sleep was more than big enough for his tiny little body. Not yet familiar with the light, since he was still to be born, he consigned himself simply to living in the midst of that darkness and, without realizing it, to slowing each step his mother took as she walked through the corridors, down the hallway, and, at times, on a clear morning, out to the pen, where she found comfort riling up the hens by stealing their chicks and hiding two or three just under her bosom, perhaps hoping that life would seem less overwhelming to her son if he heard some of the sounds of the world.

On the other hand, Crispín, despite having been inside there for eight months, had not yet opened his eyes, not even once. And one might have assumed that since he was always curled into a ball that he had not yet tried to stretch out an arm or one of his tiny legs. No, in that regard, he hadn't shown signs of life. And if it hadn't been for his heart that beat ever so softly against the wall that separated him from his mother's eyes, she would have believed that God had deceived her. And if that were the case, nothing would have stopped her from cursing Him, if only just a bit, and even then in secret.

—May the Lord forgive me—she would say to herself—, but

I'd be forced to do it, if my boy weren't alive.

Despite it all, he was very much alive. Surely he felt a bit bothered being all rolled up like a snail, and yet he lived comfortably in there, sleeping constantly while feeling, above all, protected; a sense of trust that came from the rocking motion that he felt within the large and safe cradle that was his mother.

The mother looked upon her son's presence as a solace. After all, she hadn't yet been able to rest from her tears; and there were still times when she would cling to the memory of the Crispín who had already died on her. Even now, and this was the hardest part, she hesitated to sing the one song she knew that helped children fall asleep. And yet, from time to time, she would hum it softly, as if to herself; only to be overcome quickly by a silly desire to cry, and she would weep, as only "his" absence could merit.

Afterward, she would caress her belly and ask her baby for forgiveness.

Other times, she would completely forget that her son even existed. Any little thing would end up reminding her of the other Crispín. In those moments, she would relax her eyes, let her mind wander, and simply pass the time chasing after those good memories. And it was in those inattentive moments when Crispín would strike even harder on his mother's belly, rousing her. Eventually, she would realize that the pounding of her son's heart was more than simple palpitations, it was his way of calling out to and chastising her for going so far away and leaving him all alone. With that she would blame herself for all sorts of things, not stopping until she regained her calm and lost her fear.

Because that was it, she was overwhelmed by the idea that

something might happen to her son while she let herself dream on and on about the other one. And nothing but despair seemed to fit in her head at not being able to know anything. "Perhaps he's suffering," she would say to herself. "Perhaps he's drowning in there, without any air; or maybe he's afraid of the dark. All children are frightened by the dark. All of them. And so is he. Why wouldn't he be afraid? Oh!, if only he were here on the outside, I'd know how to protect him. Or, at least I could tell if his little face were turning pale or if his eyes were becoming sad. Then I'd know what to do. But not like this; not where he's at. Not there." That's what she told herself.

Crispín existed unaware of any of that. He would simply move over a bit when he felt the emptiness that his mother's sighs created beside him. And yet those sighs actually seemed to settle him down, helping him to stay asleep, lulled as well by the steady and repetitive sound of the nearby blood as it rose and fell hour after hour.

That's how things were progressing. Other than in her worst moments, she felt quite fond about the days to come. It was even surprising to see how she was showing those signs of joy that all mothers have shortly before it happens, to help them be ready. And the way she took care of her hands, caressing them, all in the hope that she would not bruise the delicate bundle of flesh that she would soon take in her arms.

That's how things were progressing.

Nevertheless, life doesn't take itself very seriously. One would think that she already knew this, since the mother had seen life having fun with the older Crispín, playing hide and seek with him, until, eventually, the two were unable to find each other again. That's what happened. And yet, when she thought about death she always did so calmly: like a river that rises bit by bit, pushing at the old waters and slowly covering them over, but without the rushing of a new stream. That's how she imagined death, since she had seen it coming on more than once. She had seen it as well in Crispín, her husband. And although, at first, she had been unable to recognize death, when she noticed that her husband's whole body was shutting down, she didn't doubt that that's what it was.

And thus, she was fully aware of how life could treat a person, especially when one is not fully attentive.

That morning, she wanted to go to the cemetery. And since she typically would ask Crispín, the unborn one, if he agreed, that's exactly what she did this time. "Crispín," she asked, "do you think it would be alright if we went? I promise not to cry. We'll just sit a while and talk with your father, and then we'll come right back. It'll be good for both of us. What do you think?" And then, trying to guess where her son might be keeping his tiny hands: "I'll hold your hand the whole time." This is what she told him.

She opened the door to leave, but immediately felt a cold wind that was crouched low to the ground as if it were sweeping the streets. So she went back for her coat; after all, what might happen if he were to feel the cold? She looked for it among the bed linens and then in the wardrobe. She found the coat in a little corner, way up at the top. But the wardrobe was quite a bit taller than she was and so she climbed onto the first drawer. And then she placed her knee onto the second one and reached the coat with the tips of her fingers. At that moment, she imagined that Crispín had probably awakened from the strain and she rushed to get down…

She had a long way to go. Something was pushing her. And below her, the ground was far away, still out of reach…

A PIECE OF THE NIGHT

[A fragment]

Someone told me that there was an open spot along the back alley of Valerio Trujano, but that to get it I'd have to be "broken in" by the *quiebranueces*. I'd rather not say all that that entailed, since, even now, when you might say I don't have a bit of shame left, there's still something inside me that yearns to block out bad memories.

I was brand new at the time. Yet, only days after I started up, the girls of Valerio Trujano gave me a chance, making room for me right beside them. And despite how awful it was to have the guy who broke us in always hanging around, having to look at his parched face, into his waterless, eyelash-free eyes, or upon his bony carcass, it was much better to be here, working in a crowd, than to wander the streets.

Besides, in Valerio Trujano my fear went away. By the end of two or three weeks, I didn't sense it anymore, as if it had come to understand that I had grown out of it. And although I would often still feel its trembling, it would hide away when it recognized my needs, surely out of fear that I would send it to live by itself, since loneliness is the thing that fear is most afraid of, at least as far as I can tell.

It was in these circumstances that I met the guy who would later be my husband...

One night a man approached me. There was nothing unusual about this, since that's why I was there, so that men would come looking for me. But the guy who came up to me that night wasn't like the others, seeing as he was carrying a baby in his arms. A small child, one that still depends on others to get from one place to another.

When I saw him beside me, I figured he was a beggar, since he stretched out his hand as if he were asking for money. I was just about to hand over a few coins, when he asked about my price.

—No way!—I told him—. Not like this.

—What do you mean not like this?

—With that thing you've got there.

—He's not interested in that yet—he responded—. Although it wouldn't be so bad for him to start learning.

Not wanting anything to do with him, I looked around hoping to find a girl who could come over and get me out of this mess. But the few that were out were already paired off.

—Maybe you're looking for someone in particular—I said—. Someone you've been with before.

—I'm here for you—he answered—. Just tell me how much you charge.

He didn't seem to understand that I wasn't going anywhere with that little one in his arms.

—Just tell me—he repeated.

So I gave him an inflated price, maybe ten times what we normally charged.

—Okay then—he said—. ¡Vamos!

I didn't like this at all. But I also imagined that the *quiebranueces* was unlikely to give us a room at the hotel. And that's what happened. As soon as we entered the lobby, we felt the breeze created by his bony hand as he shooed us away.

—You see—I told him—, can't you see that this ain't going to happen.

—We'll be able to—he answered back—. You'll see.

We were back on the street. He put his arm around my waist and began to walk, guiding me.

—I know a place that's a bit dark... the guy in charge minds his own business. They'll let us in there.

I looked at the infant as it squirmed in his arms. It had the eyes of a grown-up, full of malice or bad intentions. I imagined that they were a perfect reflection of our iniquity.

I would have liked for it to begin howling so that the father would put this business to rest, take the baby away, and let it sleep. That's what I was thinking when the kid's eyes began to smile. He reached for me, bounced a bit, and laughed at me, showing off the solitary tooth in his mouth.

—You see?—said the guy—. He wants to be with you as well.

The child was wrapped up like a tamale, held tight in a blanket. I pressed him against my neck, patting him on the bottom so he'd go to sleep. But that kid wasn't tired; he squirmed like a worm, using his mouth to search for that place where he knew the food came from. By grabbing and pulling, he opened my blouse until his hands could take hold of my breasts.

—This kid's hungry—I told the guy.

—We've got time—he answered—. We'll get him something to eat later.

We arrived at the entrance to a hotel where he stopped me:

—Is this it?—I asked.

—Yep, right here.

We went in. We crossed a patio where bed sheets hung on a clothesline, but, as we started up the stairs, a shrill voice shouted down at us that this place was no nursery.

So we kept going, wandering around, all the way to Ogazón Street. The guy's name was Claudio Marcos. And, no, the child was not actually his. It belonged to one of his *compadres*. And he had felt compelled to take care of it since his friend was out celebrating. Well, the *compadre* did the same thing every day, but he'd never been quite so bad as now.

So that's why he took the child from the cantina, so it wouldn't keep hitting its head every time his *compadre* fell to the floor. And since the father was already wasted, it was easy to take the boy from him. The fun part would be the next day when the father comes to and can't find the youngster and has no idea where he left him.

—You're not going to take it home with you, are you?

—That's where I was headed. But I changed my mind when I saw you. It occurred to me that it might be good for the kid to spend the night with us.

—Is that your idea of fun?

—What do you mean?

—Nothing.

—I already had my eye on you—he continued—. But I couldn't get up the nerve to talk to you. With that face of yours you don't seem like the other girls. I even imagined that you might simply be passing through this area.

—So, where are we headed?—I asked.

He didn't respond. He just kept walking as he rattled on.

—You probably ought to take the boy to his mother—I told him.

—That wouldn't do any good—he responded—. She's not the one who feeds him.

We veered onto a flat, poorly lit street. When we got to the Plaza de los Ángeles, a policeman recognized who I was.

—Don't wander too far, Olga—he said.

—Who's Olga?—asked Claudio Marcos.

—I am.

—Didn't you say your name was Pilar?

—One name is as good as another. Whatever works—I answered, now a bit fed up—. What we need to do is get back. I'm quite a ways from my area.

We got to the Jardín de Santiago and sat down on a bench. The little one had fallen asleep on my shoulder. And even though he was so thin that he hardly weighed anything, I couldn't figure out how I was going to get rid of him. Nor could I explain why I was even still there, or get it through my head how we were going to sleep together, with that little one between us. And yet, the guy didn't give any sign that he wanted to end the conversation.

—Listen up—I told him, getting serious—, this boy should be asleep in his own bed by now. You ought to take him there. And if his mother won't give him her breast, then do it yourself, even if it's just to do the right thing.

—Do you think it's time for him to eat?

—I don't know—I responded—. But judging by how thin he

is I'd almost guess he'd never eaten a thing his entire life.

—Oh, no. That's not the case. I can't agree with that. The boy eats. And eats a lot. Just today at noon he finished off a half dozen tortillas. He's also fond of chilies and bean soup. He eats all that stuff. Now, if you don't believe me, let's go somewhere. I've got fifty pesos. We could find a café and get fifty pesos worth of stuff and split it between the three of us. You want to?

The truth is I was pretty hungry. We stopped at the first *tortería* we came across where, surrounded by all those people and over-whelmed by the acrid smell of fried sausage, I completely forgot what I was doing with this guy sitting there in front of me. And it occurred to me that quite some time ago he too had probably forgotten why he had picked me up off the street.

We ate. In addition to his own portion, the guy asked for a glass of milk and a few small sandwiches.

He sat the child on his legs and began feeding him one mouth-ful after another, dipped in milk. When he finished the first sand-wich, he started on the second, and did the same with the third. The boy would nibble with his one tooth, slowly working away at the bread, then he would gather it all together and swallow the whole thing all at once.

—You see how he doesn't choke?—the guy said, while laugh-ing—. His throat's that big because his parents have been stuffing him with bar food ever since he was a newborn. It's good for him to have a throat that size.

—Now that we're on the subject—I told him— what the hell are you doing with this little boy, if he has a mother to take care of him?

—Are you talking about my *comadre* Flaviana?

—I have no idea which of all your *comadres* I'm talking about. But things aren't going well for me tonight. It's embarrassing to think what I've made.

—I plan on paying you. Or would you prefer that I do it up front?

—No—I told him—, what I want is to go and look after my spot on the wall. There might be another amigo waiting for me.

The truth is that I was afraid of the *quiebranueces*. Mostly for allowing myself to be seen with a client who was carrying a child around, which surely was against the rules, but also because he must have been thinking that I was trying to pull something over on him. On top of that, there was the daily tax, something that he never forgave, even if you were coughing up blood.

The guy who claimed to be Claudio Marcos had also become lost in thought. And then he said:

—I'm a gravedigger. Does that scare you if I tell you I'm a gravedigger? Well, that's exactly what I am. And I've never admitted that my job pays a pittance. It's a job like any other. With the advantage being that I have the frequent pleasure of burying people. I'm telling you this because you, just like me, should hate people. Perhaps even more than I do. And along those lines, let me give you some advice: don't ever love anyone. Let go of the idea of caring for someone else. I remember that I had an aunt whom I really loved. She died suddenly, when I was especially attached to her, and the only thing I got out of it was a heart filled with holes.

I heard what he was saying. But that didn't take my mind off of the *quiebranueces*, with his sunken, unspeaking eyes. Meanwhile, back here, this guy just kept prattling on about how he hated half of all humankind and how great it was knowing that, one by one, he would eventually bury all those he came across every day. And how when someone here or there said or did something to offend him, he wouldn't get angry; rather, keeping his mouth shut, he would promise himself that he would give them a very long rest when they eventually fell into his hands.

—…No, I don't feel for the dead, and much less for the living. I let all of that go some fifteen years back. At first, it would make me quite sad when I had to bury a mother who had tons of kids, all of whom would break down and scream horribly and latch onto the coffin like leeches so that even the strength of three or four men wouldn't be enough to pull them away. I've seen so many cases like that. But I'm done with it. If you're going to be a gravedigger, you have to bury your compassion each time you put a body in the ground.

—…It's the living who are an embarrassment. Don't you think? The dead don't bother anyone; but then there's the living, who never stop finding ways to humiliate others. They'll almost kill themselves just to crush the soul of their fellow man. That tells you everything you need to know. On the other hand, there's no reason to hate the dead. They're great. The best people of all.

—Let's get out of here—I told him—. I feel like I'm suffocating. Let's go where we can get some air.

Back on the street, the rancid smoke of fried foods stayed with us for a while. The guy had hidden the child under his coat, surely to protect him from the night air.

—Now that you're standing, I've remembered something

else—he said—. That my *comadre* Flaviana doesn't have anything here—he explained, while rubbing his chest—. Now if she had what you've got, they'd likely be filled with *pulque*, and would be of little use in fattening up a little creature.

So I asked if he was in the habit of taking advantage of this Flaviana woman when his *compadre* spent night after night in the cantina.

He quickly said no. Since there was no way anything could ever happen seeing as she never left her husband's side.

—The two of them get plastered together and stay with each other wherever they go, until, in unison, they fall over or lose all consciousness.

I could barely listen to him. I thought about leaving to get some sleep. But he got it in his head that we should hole up for a while in some entryway, where we could be alone as if we were no longer part of the world:

—I've got this feeling that I dreamt you—he said—. Because the truth is that I've known what you looked like for quite some time now, although I like you better in my dreams... That's when I can do with you what I want. Not like now, when, as you can see, we haven't been able to do anything.

The new day was almost upon us. It smelled like morning, even though the ground, the doors, and the houses were still dark.

Weariness forced me to cross the street in search of a hotel. The guy followed behind. He stopped me:

—Do I owe you anything?

—No, nothing—I answered.

—I made you waste your time. You should charge me what you usually do for a night.

I slipped away from him. I opened the door and looked for the first vacant room. I threw myself on the bed, still dressed, closed my eyes tight, and, while letting my body relax, began to fall asleep. Someone outside was scratching at the street with a broom. Here inside someone asked:

—Will we see each other again some day? I still feel like talking with you.

I felt it when he sat down at the foot of the bed…

He's the same guy who's sitting there on the edge of my bed right now, silent, with his face buried between his hands. He just barely pulled himself away from the barred window where he tends to pass the night waiting for my return. Quite often he's told me that it's not actually me who comes home at this hour, that we'll never actually find each other:

—…or perhaps we will—he says—: maybe when I place you safely in the ground the day it becomes my job to bury you.

What he doesn't understand is that I just want to sleep. That I'm tired. It's as if he's forgotten the deal we made when I married him, that he'd let me rest. Otherwise, he'd end up losing himself in the fissures of a woman who has been devastated by the ravages of men…

A LETTER TO CLARA

Mexico City, End of February 1947

Mayecita:

They can't see the sky. They live immersed in the shadows, made darker by the smoke. They live blackened during eight hours, whether at day or at night, constantly, as if neither the sun nor the clouds existed for them to see, nor clean air for them to feel. Always just like that, unrelenting, as if they might consider resting only on the day of their death.

What I'm describing is what happens to the workers of this factory, one that's full of smoke and the smell of crude rubber. And yet I'm still supposed to keep an eye on them, as if the watching of these machines that don't know the peace of a deep breath weren't enough. That's why I imagine I won't last long being the kind of boss they want me to be. Just the thought of working like that makes me sad and resentful. And only the thought that you exist takes away the sadness and the horrible bitterness.

After seeing things here I couldn't imagine existed, I'm starting to believe that my heart is a tiny balloon filled with pride that's easily deflated. Perhaps I'm just incapable of explaining it all to you, but more or less what I mean is that in this strange world men are machines and machines are considered men.

But I'm talking about things that don't have anything to do with you, and that's not right. It took me until now to find an envelope I could use to send you your photographs. They don't let us out of work until five in the afternoon and this place where I find myself, me who's head over heals for you and dying little by little, is a fair way from the center of town. And everything closes there at five. That's just the way things are. I made more copies of each of the three photos that I'm sending you, but I'm not giving you more than one of each out of fear that you might go crazy handing them out to all of those boyfriends you have. It might be a few days before they get the other ones to me, the ones that you picked out.

On the other hand, I can't imagine how such a tiny little wisp of a girl can USE SUCH HUGE LETTERS when writing a letter. That's quite a trick.

Nonetheless, your letter cheered me up. I used both hands to grab it and I used both of my eyes to read it, and then I read it again because there's something there that makes my heart happy. There's something in everything about you that makes my heart very happy. And you know that we need to keep this heart that I've given over to you content.

Remember that you're the one who would give me apples and not me. And don't forget that it was Eve who gave Mr. Adam a piece of an apple, giving birth to the custom that women have of giving away apples.

I haven't been to the movies here. They just aren't any good without you. It isn't even fun to arrive late and not find a seat.

Those inconveniences were amusing and it would almost be worth coming home just for them.

I still haven't moved to a new place, but I think I'll do that next month. I'll look for a house with birds just like the ones you have, ones that hardly sing, nor jump, because of how old they are, and yet are still birds in the end. I believe if I like you so much it must be because of that, because there's a bit of bird in you; it could be your eyes or your quiet little mouth that I love so much.

I haven't gone anywhere either, even though the two Sundays I've spent here were great days to make a quick trip to climb Ajusco or to say hello to the Popo, that volcano that seems to feel as alone and abandoned as this hard-headed young man who would love to love you more than he already loves you.

I've gone to visit Uncle David and Aunt Teresa; Aunt Julia and Aunt Julia's children, including Venturina, the one you know; Uncle Raúl and Aunt Rosa… I've shown your pictures to all of them. They asked me where you were from. They just can't imagine that here, on this big wide world, that something so ugly and spine chilling as you could be born and raised and live. They can't believe it and that's because they've stopped being like little children and to stop being like a little child is to no longer believe in God's little angels. That's what's happened to them.

"To begin again." Oh, how I'd love to be living there and be able to meet you again for the first time, but unafraid, without complications, and without any fear of losing you.

It's just that living here is not easy. It's as if everything is new and you have to learn how to live all over again. At times I imagine that I've been sick ever since I came to this city and that I'll never get better. And I feel as if the current of a river were dragging me along, as if I were being pushed forward, as if I weren't allowed to look back.

You know what, Chachinita, I've thought about washing my hands of Goodrich. Just the thought made me feel more relaxed; but they've arranged things so that it's impossible for me to do it. It's as if they have me shackled to my relatives, and more so all the time, as if their sole purpose were to take care of me. And now I understand why I never liked asking for favors, and it's because I don't like accepting them.

At times I wish they would all just leave me alone, that they wouldn't give me the peace of mind of knowing that they could help out at a moment's notice. That they would just let me know that I can't count on them. That way I'd be all alone. And perhaps on my own, without relying on anyone, I could know what I need to do. And with just your help perhaps I could find the path that would let me do what I should do.

Next to my mother, the only woman whom I have to thank for having done something for me, is you. I don't want to have to thank anyone else for anything. I feel better that way, knowing that I don't owe anyone any favors. I feel less miserable and less desperate knowing that I don't have to please many people. That's my way of thinking, my pretty little girl. But reality is different. It's hard and it makes you feel its toughness and give in, unless you want to go crazy trying to find a way out.

What I'm describing is the environment in which I've lived since I began at the factory. Never had I seen so much stuff in one place; so much effort united to finish off the human spirit; to make men see that ideals are superfluous, that thoughts and love are strange things. That's why I've asked for your comfort, since you're the only one who can give it to me and help me feel more at peace, so I'll stop rebelling against everything that goes against who I am. I once asked for your help and I need it now, since we're fighting for the two of us, to make our own world together, the one I know exists, because I have already lived in it. A world where no one causes someone else to be afraid or to become resentful. And you and I can create that.

This letter is born out of an immense indignation that they've made me endure. Sometime later I'll tell you the source of that indignation. How it made me feel is what I'm trying to explain for now. And my conclusion is that a person should live in that place where he feels happiest. Life is short and then we are buried for such a long time.

I hope you'll scold me for writing to complain rather than speaking of the love that I have for you, but I had to tell someone about what I'm feeling. And you were born to hear my confessions. Perhaps a bit later I'll even get around to telling you my sins.

I hope that you're well and prettier than anyone else (I was going to say: as pretty as ever, but then I remembered how sometimes you can turn very ugly, like when you get after me). And I hope that everyone there etc., etc.

I send to you, my sweet little darling, all of the affection of the one who loves you and who hopes to love you more, along with a huge and tender hug and many kisses, many of them, all coming from the one who will love you always.

Juan

P.S. I wasn't going to send you this letter because of how sad it is. But since two other versions that I wrote were just as bad, I've decided to send it just as it is and not delay writing you any longer. I suggest you don't pay me any attention, since I'm just a guy who loves to complain.

Tu muchacho

CASTILLO DE TEAYO

A lantern brings us to a stop. A red lantern whose light fans out and sways in front of us. The lantern is all that's visible. The rain and the night close the roadway. "What do they want? Where are we?"

The lantern approaches and someone, from the other side of the darkness, tells us: "Lower your lights! Please! Pull to the side!"

The automobile fogs up with the rain. It jerks. It backs up a bit and moves off the asphalt into the ditch. It stops there.

The rain falls a bit harder now, in white sheets, mixed in with the mist.

A strange copper-like face pokes through the open window: "You can't go any farther —it says. The retaining wall in Mata Oscura has collapsed. The road's closed. That's it. You can head back to Poza Rica or stay here. Whatever you prefer."

He's a soldier. Behind him, water runs down a rifle in radiant drops.

—Where are we? What is this place?

Nothing. The soldier has disappeared.

A clearing forms in the fog. An opening through which an orange light enters as if morning were breaking, coming from behind us. That's Poza Rica. We're not far. I get out of the automobile. The steering wheel has been in my hands for hours.

It feels moist and slips in the wet heat. In the rain I pass by a long line of cars and trucks that seem to be in a deep sleep, leaning into the ditch. I head toward the lantern. I ask:

—The collapse…?

—How can I help you —he interrupts.

—… is it past Tihuatlán or before it?

—Past it. In Mata Oscura.

—Well then. Let us by. We're headed to Tihuatlán.

—This is Tihuatlán —and he points to his left, toward the black night. This is it right here.

—We can keep going then…, right?

—Not through there. Through here you can. Like I said.

The rain begins to clear. The headlights on the car search toward the left and discover a few houses among the bushes. On one side, a puddle-filled road.

—Is this the way?

—The road to Álamo. Sí señor.

—But we're headed to Castillo de Teayo.

—It's the same thing. Up ahead is the turn-off.

We start up. We advance slowly through the potholes for a long stretch, being careful. The clouds were low and a blue mist rose out of the ground. We hoped that it wouldn't rain again. A few men passed by.

—Where's the turn-off to the Castillo?

They pointed toward a grass house.

—Over there.

—Good. Thanks a lot.

We left the white of the dirt road and dropped down onto a

dark pathway. The car kept going a bit longer through the mud. Then it slid back and forth before coming to a stop, trembling as if someone were shaking it.

We got out to look. Mud had gotten into everything. That car wasn't going anywhere. We closed the doors. We still had 14 kilometers to go to get to Castillo de Teayo. Our destination.

We walked. Searching with our feet for any patch of grass, we followed the trail, probing the mud; slipping and wobbling like gray shadows lost in the gray mist.

The rainforest could be seen all around us. The tall ceiba trees, disjointed, poking through now and again. The parota trees driving their roots toward the road. Otate reeds. Grumbling about things. *Palapas* made of quiet palm leaves, motionless under the weight of so many clouds. Everywhere you could hear the croaking of the frogs and, above all else, the screaming of the crickets. Everything was filled with that unrelenting noise without any silence. All around us, dense, still dripping with water, the Huasteca rainforest… Heavy drops of rain that sounded as they fell like cracking tree branches. Without any smell of the earth. Just the mighty, abundant, and ancient green smell of the rainforest.

We moved quickly toward the west, as if the night were pushing us on. The heat was getting stronger. There was no breeze. The fog fell and rose and opened up in small fractures. Then it would make everything dark again. And it was like that for more than an hour. For more than two hours.

Everyone was asleep in Castillo de Teayo. It seemed a ghost town.

We sat down and, with our feet stiff from fatigue, we waited for the day, huddled in an entryway, all the while listening to the nearby sound of the gloomy Huasteca Sea.

Just before sunrise a northern breeze began to blow. The fog came in, pulled along by the wind. When the fog cleared, clouds continued to pass overhead, dropping rain in torrents, closing the horizon. As the wind blew stronger the mass of clouds gained altitude and pressed on, heavy and slow, toward the mountains.

A pale, yellowish gleam appeared in the east, revealing the outlines of everything. Meanwhile, on the side of the mountain, the world remained gray, increasingly gray and invisible.

Then, right in front of our eyes, was the Castillo. Its shape was strange in its seclusion, still undisturbed by any sign of life. It was surrounded by a mist that rose like steam from the humid earth and the dampened walls smoothed over with moss. With the moss covered in dew. That's what we saw.

Night had come to an end.

That's when that guy appeared, tall, thin, with his shirt open and a beard swarming around him in the wind. He stopped in front of us and began to speak:

—This is where the gods came to die. The banners were destroyed in the ancient wars and the standard-bearers fell to the ground, their noses broken and their eyes blinded, buried in the mud. Grass grew over their backs and even the nauyaca snake built its nest in the hollow of their curled legs. They're here again, but without their banners, once again enslaved, once again guardians, now watching over the wooden cross of Christianity. They seem solemn, their eyes dull, their jaws dropped, their mouths open, clamorous beyond measure. Someone has whitewashed their bodies, giving them the appearance of the dead, wrapped in shrouds and ripped from their graves.

The man is the one who speaks. We listen. That tall, long-legged man, who seems so full of rage.

I'll take you to the rocks—he tells us.

And we go with him. With him up front, us behind. We walk along a creek bed made of large, well-polished stones.

—They built the Castillo with these stones. They were also used to make the images of the gods. Up ahead we'll see how they made use of these stone slabs to draw stories and to make so many other things that no longer exist.

That's what the guy was telling us.

Under the zalate trees, at the edge of a ravine overgrown with vegetation, was the great stone. Dark green ferns were growing along its edges, as well as in those spots where the sun never reaches. And along a smooth surface, extending almost to the ground, were some figures carved in relief. Perhaps a priest guiding his pilgrims or an army adorned with feathers heading off to its defeat.

—After all, where else did these men go but to their defeat? They were victorious at times. They spread their victory all the way to the sea. But ultimately their footprints were wiped away, expunged by the final destiny that waited for them, before the end of their lives.

"And this is a story that isn't to be understood, but rather to sense that they wanted to leave something everlasting, at least."

—That's good. Yes, that's good—we said.

—This one's not alone. There are a lot of them. Some have been removed, but many are still here. They'll be here forever. On those hills, on those over there, and on those other ones there are many more. We've unearthed a few of them and they're still there. Here you might say that in no time they'll be covered over again, since the forest multiplies and thrives from one day to the next, constantly putting on weight like an animal. I'd take you to see them if it weren't for the ticks. Let's head back.

Here's the Castillo again. The light of the sun, now under an open sky, shines on its walls and on its steps rounded by the years.

Some kids are playing on the platform. Today is a nice day. The last northern storm has passed and it'll be at least a week before bad weather returns.

Someone is singing over there under the entryway: "*Yo tenía mi cascabel…*" It reminds us that we're in Veracruz.

But the man's voice returns us to the past, and we cross again back through time.

—Take a look. Here they are. Those are the gods of the Huastecos. Notice the plumes of feathers fanned out over their heads. Look at their eyes. Those are Huasteco eyes. Their noses are gone. They were cut off by the enemy. That was the sign of defeat. That one is called Centeocíhuatl; she's the goddess of germination and rain. This other one is her as well. Perhaps they came here from different regions, gathering here to die. Because they're dead. Can you tell? They're just worthless stones now.

And he points to an idol, bent over, that is now part of a fence that forms a corral near someone's house.

—I'd love to tell you the name of each one; of this one or that one, but I don't know them. No one here knows their names. But they must have names. If men have names, all the more reason for the gods to have them. But I don't know them. That one is Centeocíhuatl, that's all I know.

"I also know that this is where the very best of the Huastecos lived. This Castillo was the center of their sacred city. Closing your eyes you can imagine the great *teocali* and the lesser temples scattered throughout the valley. With their venerated gods at the very top, now sacrificed. This secluded spot was discovered by Mexica patrols and its men were subdued. And yet, because they feared their gods, they kept looking after them.

"Once there had been many wars. And the wars between the Huastecos and the Totonacos were endless. Not bloody, but long. One might say that they had lasted since the beginning of time.

At Tapamanchoco, at the edge of the lagoon, lies the burial ground of the lost warriors. And at Tabuco, by the sea, the funerary urns where they cremated the priests. Every man and woman had his or her place in this kingdom. A place to live and to die.

"Tuxpan and Chicontepec, and Tihuatlán here a bit closer, were all overrun many times by the waves of Totonaco military campaigns. And Castillo de Teayo was cut off, defenseless, completely in their control. And this was because the Huastecos were often inebriated, leading to their demise, making them unfit to fight. After some time, a counterattack was launched and the Totonacos fled, hiding in the Papantla rainforest. That's how the Huastecos were able to recover their village, but not without finding their gods with their noses cut off.

"All of this came to an end when the Mexicas took control of Cempoala, far to the south, hitting at the very heart of the Totonacos. And almost immediately they fell on Teayo, turning this location into a military outpost. Something like a wedge splitting the two kingdoms, all to better divide and defeat them more quickly.

"But it wasn't the Mexicas that left this like it is now. They weren't the ones who killed off the gods, pulling them down from their altars, breaking them apart, and scattering them like useless stones. No, one day the Mexicas just left to defend their own lands and never returned. The ones who put an end to the gods of Teayo were those who were called a 'people of reason' and they conquered these lands...

"... Then time passed. An absence of faith. Because the absence of faith is the same as a lack of blood in one's veins.

"So, when our fathers came here to live, bringing us along to inhabit this place, there was a fully grown ceiba tree on top of the Castillo, and that's all I need to say, since we're right in the middle of the rainforest and the jungle is always growing and advancing, growing fat hour after hour."

That's what the man told us. And we listened to him while sitting on top of the Castillo de Teayo, under the bells, since this is what now serves as the town's bell tower.

From this height you can look out over the entire valley. The idols are down below. A few resting, others standing, some lying scattered on the ground. It's mid-morning and the smell of the wild mint plants penetrates as it rises to meet us.

CASTILLO DE TEAYO, PHOTOGRAPHS BY JUAN RULFO

Carved Stone on Road,
Castillo de Teayo

Leaning Figure,
Castillo de Teayo

Sculpted Relief,
Castillo de Teayo

Female Figure,
Castillo de Teayo

Pyramid,
Castillo de Teayo

AFTER DEATH

I died not long ago. I died yesterday. For all of you, yesterday means ten years ago. For me, it's just a few hours. Death is immutable in space and time. It's just death, without contradiction, not standing in contrast to absence or to presence. It's a place where neither life nor the void exists. All that is born out of me, is the transformation of my very self. The worms that have chewed on my flesh, that have pierced my bones, that pass through the sockets of my eyes and the recesses of my mouth and eat at the ends of my teeth, have all died and have given birth from within their own bodies to other worms that have devoured my flesh that has turned to stench and that stench has transformed even the eternities into life's pestilences, into life's humiliations. But death has not gained ground. I'm here, surrounded by the earth, in the very spot where they buried me forever.

I don't have feelings. Only memories. Bad memories. Whatever little bit of good there was in me went to heaven with my soul, in the last tear to fall from my eyes.

Let me give you some advice. When you go to die, cry. Use any means necessary to make yourself shed a tear, even if it's only one. That's the path that the soul takes. Do everything you can to push your soul out of your body, because if you don't you'll suffer the most severe and insufferable pain that is given to man.

I met a dead man not long ago who had locked up his soul. He told me that he had been buried alive, half dead. He had to face death from inside his own tomb, racked with hatred, seething, writhing about in desperation, feeling his blood springing from his eyes, blinded by blood and by terror. He held on to his soul, there in the darkness of death.

—I thought I was in hell—he told me—. I entered the throes of death as if I were entering hell, into that intense and eternal fire that they tell us about on earth. Each insignificant pore of my body burned in its own flame. My bones turned to ash and I kept languishing in death, aware of the corporeal existence, making sense of my destructive process; but living still as a human being lives. An internal force caused me pain; it steadied itself and beat on the walls that were already coming apart, and I collapsed exhausted, lifeless, as if finally I had found some rest. But rest for the soul is found in hell or in heaven, not in the human body. That which for humans is purgatory, is nothing but a prison for the soul because of the body. Until at last the water in my eyes turned to tears. The pain made me sob, or maybe I was no longer aware of the pain, perhaps on account of how intense my dying was. I only know that I relaxed. I no longer posses that soul that made me suffer. Now I'm at peace.

That's what that guy told me.

And one other thing. Don't make others weep. It's a rebuke that endures and that weighs on those who have died. It vanishes among the living, but lives on among the dead, because death is forever.

MY AUNT CECILIA

I reckon that I've forgotten many things, but I haven't forgotten the afternoon that my Aunt Cecilia died. I was next to her bed, seated in a chair, watching her raise her arms every now and then as if to defend herself from the illness that was afflicting her and that she had been battling since dawn.

I remember that she would shake her arms like a blind person searching in the darkness for that thing causing the pain. Then she would rest. She would stretch her legs and rest. The only sound I heard was the raspy breathing coming from her mouth like bubbling air. Surely an unhealthy air, because her lips resonated as she breathed.

I think about the time that has gone by since the day that she died, since when she passed I was left all alone. She, whom while alive had been so anxious to look after me, had completely forgotten to entrust me with someone who would take care of me when she died. I was ten years old at the time. And no, she didn't place me in anyone's care.

I remember that very night how I woke up alone after everyone had left. I was sitting next to my Aunt Cecilia's bed, and she was there as well, watching me with open eyes that never turned away, as if through them, she hoped to tell me something that would help me to never be afraid.

I remember that because, when I closed her eyes with my fingers, it seemed as if the light had gone out forever and that everything was filled with darkness.

I am lying in that same bed of hers, where she unfurled her body so that death wouldn't have to work so hard to take her, and I think about how she shouldn't have died so suddenly, knowing that I would be the one to suffer without her around any more.

At times I think that she shouldn't have loved me the way she loved me only to leave so abruptly as if there weren't anything left for her to worry about; and, it's worse when one could see even through closed eyes that I would suffer after finding her gone. She misjudged things alright. And I think she should've fought a bit harder, let's say another hour or two; finding some way to hang on, and she could've used that time to wash her hands of me, telling me something that would make me hold a grudge that might endure until now.

But she did the opposite. It's as if she set out to find strength in the way she expressed herself, a force that I would recognize and that I liked to see in her. It also seems that she wanted to pass that strength on to me in a way that would last forever, like a gift that she was offering me so that life would never frighten me. That's what I imagine now. I imagine that's what my Aunt Cecilia wanted to tell me with her eyes, looking for the easiest way to say it.

And if someone hadn't come to close them and tell me: "She's no longer here," I never would have moved, because I wouldn't have, because I knew that that look of hers was the same one she would use when she would let loose the affection that she had for me.

CLEOTILDE

I was already thoroughly blistered with bitterness; and yet she would make it all disappear just by looking my way and allowing me to gaze upon her. And it's because to look at a woman the way you would want to look at her, without anything between her and you, other than the vision of one's eyes, can drive you crazy and make you suddenly lose your voice. That had to affect me deeply. That's what I believe.

You've always been alone. All of those close to you passed away quite some time ago and you've wandered through the world coming undone just as a single tiny tear from a cloud falls apart in the wind. You end up losing and then losing again, little by little, the hope of finding what you need to be strong, until suddenly it appears with arms that are riddled with holes, with eyes like water; with that way of holding you tight and letting go, showing you in passing how not to feel ashamed.

I've been staring at the wall for a good while now thinking about what I've just told you and thinking about how I might work everything out so that she, my Aunt Cecilia, could still be alive. But no, no one is alive; not even my father who lived right here and who I never got to know; nor my mother, nor anyone else. The only things on the wall are chips of paint that are peeling off and smudges from something that someone tossed over there some time ago.

Where I don't want to look is toward the ceiling, because up on the ceiling, moving from beam to beam, there's someone who's alive. Especially at night, when I light a small candle, that shadow on the ceiling moves. Don't think it's just a figment of my imagination. I know what it is: it's the shape of Cleotilde.

Cleotilde is also dead, but not fully so. Even though I'm the one who killed Cleotilde. And I know that everything you kill, while you remain alive, continues to exist. That's just how it is.

It's been about a week since I killed Cleotilde. I hit her several times on the head, massive and hard blows, until she stayed good and quiet. It's not like I was so mad that I was planning on killing her; but a fit of rage is a fit of rage and that's the root cause of it all. She died. Afterward, I did get mad at her for that, for having died. And now she's after me. That's her shadow, above my head, spread along the length of the beams as if it were the shadow of a barren tree. And even though I've told her many times to go away, to stop harassing everyone, she hasn't moved from where she's at, nor has she stopped looking at me.

I'm not sure exactly where she's looking right now; yet I imagine she's staring at me not just with her eyes, but with every bit of her shadow and, at times, it seems as if she's still oozing blood since I've felt a few black drops fall from her head, as if someone were wringing out her hair.

Cleotilde had a beautiful and radiant head of hair. Sometimes I dream that I'm still lying by her side, with my face buried in her hair that was so smooth that it would make me forget about everything, even her. And it wouldn't have bothered me if Cleo-tilde had left my side whenever she wanted, if only she would've left me with her hair so I could bury my face in it and soak my hands in strands that seemed as soft as water.

In any case, that's how it happened. While she was with me I had what I most wanted. But lately she had made herself scarce, showing up only every now and again, and then at the break of dawn. As a result, I wasn't able to savor again the most incredible sensation I have ever known.

Then I killed her. I've had more than enough time to repent: a full week of days and nights without sleep during which I could've repented many times over. And if I weren't constantly dwelling on the moment I killed her, I could already have extracted the remorse needed for her to leave me in peace.

But as it happens I think about that day constantly. I barely have time to think about anything else, so much so that my fingernails have grown longer while all I do is turn that day over and over in my head; not the moment when I killed her, rather a bit earlier, when I tried to stroke her hair and she got mad.

That's what I think about. About the face that she pulled and what she said to me. Ah! If only she hadn't said anything, my anger would've dosed off, as it had done many times before, fully sub-dued by shame and I simply wouldn't have had the grit to kill her.

And yet, even though nearly four months had passed since she had last slept with me and she had no right to be angry, she still got mad. She became as irritable as a wasp when I asked her to lie down at my side. She was my wife and she should offer me her body when I had need of it. She told me:—You're a slobbering mess!

So I dried my mouth on the corner of the sheet.

—You pig! Your Aunt Cecilia must've raised you in her loins—she ended up saying. And then she drove her words home with a slap to my face.

Her words hung there silent for quite awhile, spattered on my face. Why'd she bring my Aunt Cecilia into it? What had my Aunt Cecilia ever done for her to speak that way about her, huh? What had she done? I got up from the bed.

—Maniac!—she yelled at me—. Abuser of the dead!

I took two or three steps. I returned to bed and saw Cleotilde up close. Had she really said that my Aunt Cecilia was this and that? Who was Cleotilde to speak ill of my Aunt Cecilia? Did she really not know...?

I grabbed Cleotilde by the hair and she became enraged.

—Let go of me, you damn madman!

But I had already grabbed her with both of my hands. I threw her out of bed. She was dressed as if she were going out. Only her feet were uncovered. I heard how her feet bounced when they hit the ground together. In her loins! What exactly were you suggesting when you said that?

I grabbed the bar we used to secure our door and I slammed it against Cleotilde's head. She folded over like a broken chair: "¡Pobrecita de mí!," she was able to say in a partially numb voice.

After that I wasn't sure why I kept hitting her. I saw the bar fall and rise as if it were something that wasn't in my hands. I saw my clenched fists, with veins that were swollen and darkened with blood. And I felt that the warm mist coming from Cleotilde's head was peppering my eyes, blinding me.

By the time my anger settled back into place and I was once again able to clearly see what was going on around me, Cleotilde was already dead. I crouched down to look at her and, squatting by her side, I just stared and stared for a good while at that balled up mass that moved every now and then, while small streams of battered blood flowed from its nose and mouth.

That's when I understood how frail her life had been and how little effort it had taken for me to break it. I never imagined it would be so easy to kill someone. That came to me when I saw Cleotilde without any hope left, with her arms sagging and her body limp, as if everything had fallen apart on her.

I never expected it to be so easy to die. No. She wasn't supposed to die. I only wanted to scare her. Give her a good scare so she would lose the desire to go around sullying the name of my Aunt Cecilia and to see, if in that way, she would behave better, and stop coming home at such late hours of the night, still savoring traces of the man with whom she had been sleeping. I didn't want things to keep on like that. My skin wasn't thick enough to put up with that forever and she must have known what was going to happen in time. I had already told her that once.

At that time I spoke apprehensively, with soft words, almost as if I was talking in a way that wouldn't end up making her mad. I told her:

—Look here, Cleotilde, I'm already old. I've just turned fifty-nine and as you can imagine I don't need much from you, of that which is yours; but I would like for that little bit that you do give me every now and then to be given passionately. You can't imagine how much I love the passion you put into those things that you do. Truly you wouldn't be able to get your head around how much I love it. Nonetheless, you don't even want to give me that courtesy. You go out with those other guys. Do you think I don't know where you are when you disappear all night? I know quite well, Cleotilde. You've been in this and that place, with this and that guy. I've seen you at Pedro's house, sleeping with him, laughing at the tickling that he knows how to give you with his tongue, and I've seen you as well with Florencio, that guy who rents barrel organs. And with many more, Cleotilde, with many more whom I barely know who they are. But I've never complained to you. Isn't it true that I've never complained about anything? When I've thought about doing so, I've told myself: "You can't complain about the chayote plant because it will give you chayotes full of worms." That's what I've told myself and I've kept my mouth shut. Also, what would I gain by getting after you? You would leave me forever. That's the only thing I'd get by being strict with you and it pains me to sit and think that you might leave me, just like that, to never return. I do know that in that case I would feel genuinely lost, not having you around.

I kept telling her other things. There was a time when I even considered telling her I didn't mind if she amused herself with the others, nor if she thought of them when she was in my arms. It seemed like I told her some of that. That's how appalling my thinking was. And it's because I loved her. You could see from miles away how much I was in love with Cleotilde. Despite all that, I promised her then that I would calm her down if she didn't get better on her own. Or at least I tried to tell her that. I didn't threaten her, as you can see; my intention was to encourage her to mend her own ways. But she didn't do that. Now she began cutting into even that little bit of the night that she used to spend with me until it disappeared completely. She wouldn't even make it back on time to see the sun come up from her own bed. And that bed became cold with only myself there, with only me, since my presence wasn't enough to warm it without her there.

The first days I was happy just to hear her footsteps. I would open my eyes and keep quiet without breathing, hoping to hear her feet approaching. I made do with that. She would arrive and lie down in the same spot as always, taking off whatever she had on, without covering herself with anything but her arms. And then she would sleep. My eyes would lose their own drowsiness just by watching how Cleotilde slept; watching as sleep wandered around her knees, relaxing her from her toes to the joints of her legs, approaching and then satisfying her belly, seeing it rise from within her breasts and softly pass over them until they too drifted off, until suddenly, it would take her over completely, leaving her only with the silent air of her breathing, that rise and fall as if it were a vapor filling her and drawing the weariness out. I covered myself in the delicate blue light of daybreak and watched her, and I made do with that. I would have liked, at times, to take her by one of her hands and stay with her forever; but that would have been difficult. She wanted me to let her sleep. She didn't want me pawing at her. She was fed up with pawing and with everything else. "Control yourself!," she would say to me. "I've had it up to here!" And she would point to her neck.

She had just come from being with Pedro or with some other guy. So I didn't touch her. I devoured her with my eyes, but I hid my hands so they wouldn't try anything on their own. I positioned them beneath the pillow, close together, each one keeping the other in check, in case one of them couldn't resist the urge to touch that blue body there at my side. Then I waited, hoping that Cleotilde might feel the need to hold on to something.

Lately, that need just hadn't shown up. Her mood seemed somber and drained. And it's because Pedro or someone else with whom she had spent the night had left her useless. That's what was going on.

It takes a lot of effort for me to get mad now for not having gotten mad then about what Cleotilde was doing to me. She didn't count on how miserable I was for turning a blind eye. On top of that, she would place herself right in front of my eyes, squinting and watchful as if they were gazing full of love, but without seeing anything of the sort, and she would entice me closer with the naked heat of her body, as if she were trying to more fully stir up my evil intentions.

—Don't come close to me!—she would say with her tongue already rolling around in a dream.

She provoked me into doing something bad. And I did it. It's been a week since I killed her. I took the bar we use to secure the door and I pounded it hard on her head. That's how she died. Afterwards I cried. I bent over to look at her up close and seeing her in the state she was in, I cried. She must have cried as well, because I remember very well how I took out my handkerchief to clean the tears that were coming out of the corners of her eyes. Shortly afterward, I opened the door and left.

Now there won't be anyone who hates us.

I got as far as where the trees are and I sat her down next to a trunk. There was a lot of moss and she would be comfortable there even if it were for a long time. Then I crossed her hands on her legs, I dried her wet eyes with a rag, and I let her sleep. I imagined that she would rest. I thought that I had treated her poorly and that now she would rest and fall asleep in that quiet spot on top of that moss that was so soft.

I didn't speak with her at all. By then she had been dead for quite awhile and she wouldn't have been able to hear me.

MY FATHER

My father was a good man.

He lived in that era when everything was bad. When no one was able to make plans for what was to come, since what was to come was uncertain and the here and now had not yet ended. Times were bad: you couldn't catch sight of heaven or earth; nor if the sun were out or if the wind was coming from the north or the south. Everything was bad in the world. But my father was good and he believed in life.

They killed him at dawn one morning, but he failed to notice when he died or why. They killed him and for him life was over. It continued to exist for others and little by little calm returned to the world, and life began to renew itself until even the moisture of rain was visible, distracting everyone and restoring a sense of hope.

My father died on a dark morning, without the least bit of splendor, among the shadows. They wrapped him in a sheet as if he were just anyone and buried him beneath the ground just as they do with all men. "You're father has died," they told us, in that moment of awakening when things don't hurt; when children are born, when they put to death those who are sentenced to die. In that hour of slumber when you find yourself in the middle of a sleep that is filled with dreams that are of little worth and yet bearable, terrible but necessary.

—Your father has died.

I was dreaming that I was holding a deer in my arms. A sleeping deer, as small as a bird without wings; tepid as a heart that calmly beats, but drowsy.

—His life is over.

It was dawn, so dark, so lacking in color, without any color. When everything is so far away.

And I had to cry, had to wring my heart for it to give up its juice. Coerce it until it sobbed. Coerce a heart that still dreams and remains somewhat asleep, only to pound it with the hammer of sorrow and make it feel it's own pain. That's what I did, merely to cry. To not groan in silence.

"The deer has died. It's just a dead animal lying in your arms."

Let me continue my dream. Everything else is a lie. No one can die while you're asleep.

—It's three in the morning and we've brought your father. They murdered him last night.

Last night. Which night? My life doesn't have a night. It's not dark. Life always exists during the day. What are you saying?

—That it's three in the morning. Get up. You're father's here, laid out. They murdered him last night.

—Who? Are you talking about my father? He can't die. No one can do anything to him. Justice would destroy the earth. It would dry up all the hands and make life useless for men. He has given us life and if we feel like there is day it's because of him, and if we feel that there is life it's because of him. He can't die.

—They've killed him.

—When? At what time?

I didn't feel anything, and the world would have felt it.

—Last night. Get up. Come see him.

—It's a lie.

—They're going to bury him in the afternoon.

—They're not going to bury anyone. My father can't be a dead man. He'll die after us. His life isn't one that's full of misery like ours, nor of scraps as ours is…

—Aren't you going to see him? Get up and come see him before the other people who loved or knew him get here.

—My father hasn't died. You hate me. You're here to wake me because you hate me. Let me finish my dream.

—Whatever you want, but after midday they're going to bury him.

—Turn off the light. Turn off that light and leave. Why are you laughing if you say my father has died? Leave. I've got a sleeping deer here. Don't wake him. I know who you are. I know that only the devil gets up early to frighten those who sleep. He hasn't died, that's a complete lie. That's an absolute lie. Get out of here!

Then my cry turned liquid like blood. And when I heard the wailing of my mother off in the distance, my blood became like water.

SAME AS YESTERDAY

"Same as yesterday," said the father. "The same smile."

He gathered his things and returned to continue Mass. His head moved back and forth, paying no mind to his body's movement. And suddenly he realized he was thinking about his body. Or perhaps not about his but rather about that of Susana San Juan, who had revealed her naked breasts, floating in the warm air, and the beginning of her waist, there where all the sins of men are sewn.

But he was not a man. He had been once, but now he belonged to a different humanity. He shook his head to erase the image of that woman: beloved woman, beautiful with a clean beauty. And again those breasts that floated in the air sustained by a breath. Those breasts, cradle of love. But he had no claim on them, or on anything else. He cleared his head again and entered the Gospel side of the church, blessing the faithful with trembling hands. Then he sank back into an intense memory, recent, while his hands, relying on the tips of his fingers, reviewed the letters of the Mass, not daring to look upon the whole page. Those letters, having the shape of a woman. Then, overcome by swollen veins, he uttered the name of Susana San Juan and closed his eyes as he trembled at just the name. He uttered it again as a form of self-chastisement, believing it to be a whip of fire that could part his face and, at that very moment, he again distinguished breasts among the rounded letters.

He knelt for the Eucharist, modeling the gestures of Christ's prayer in the garden. But he closed the chalice without having taken of the body or the blood. He followed the movements haltingly, holding his breath, waiting for a sign of rebuke. And while listening to the sound of the church bells, he assumed that the faithful would be bowed toward the ground with their eyes closed and he forgave himself, since he felt repentant in his intent.

Swallows entered the church through an open door and passed through the nave. He heard their chirping in the silence that precedes the culmination of the Mass: the prayer given in Latin, in a language that can illuminate or be transformed into an unintelligible murmur.

He closed the breviary and entered the Gospel of Saint John: "In the beginning was the Word." But by then the faithful had already abandoned the church that was barely illuminated at this hour, barely visited by a handful of old women, useless, up at the crack of dawn because of old age and sleeplessness. He thought of Susana and rubbed his hands together to give the blessing.

—Father Villalpando. Sebastián Villalpando… You can see him, over there, next to the hill, where the fifteen crosses are. One of them belongs to him. He died for the cause on April 23, 1927.

He picked up the stole that had fallen and thought about the hot chocolate, about the cookies. He said: "We are all human after all." He thought about the *requesón* cheese and about the frothy milk. But then all of a sudden a fully nude body appeared next to him, right in front, and he looked at it. He leaned against the pillar of the parish and his hands embraced the image while his burning lips kissed the fresh lime plaster where the body of Susana was drawn. "I don't understand why," he said. "I don't understand why." And water dropped from his lips that bit into the smooth trunk of a pillar made of a single piece of stone.

Later, when he pulled himself away, he said: "I have a full day in front of me, but I don't know what'll happen when night falls."

When night came they called for him again. He went. He wrapped the Holy Oils in the folds of his shirt, to not attract attention, to not worry the town.

"I don't want you to follow me with the bell," he told the sacristan. "It's best that no one find out."

This took place on the eve of the Feast of the Immaculate Conception. A Saturday, the seventh of December.

SUSANA FOSTER

The rain leapt as it hit the water of the stream, forming small bubbles that were carried away by the current. Some burst, others disappeared in dew-spattered ripples. The entire stream bubbled up creating a lather that sounded like the song of crickets hidden in the grass.

Muddy threads slowly emerged in the translucent water, as if red streamers had fallen into the creek. As small streams dropped through ancient channels, they gathered up the loose soil that had formed from chamomile leaves, from old saffron leaves, and from ripened thyme, all made red from the color of the dirt. The water became cloudy, turning increasingly red and gray and black, growing dark until the sand on the bottom disappeared in the shadows.

At that moment, Susana Foster closed her eyes. Her body felt pleasant, naked beneath the tepid summer that began to sow the earth. The cleansing breeze of the rain fell in fresh waves over her muscles, on her arms, and around her breasts. Her eyelids, closed to the light, sensed the new era, and her eyes, there inside, smiled, as only Susana Foster's eyes knew how.

★

—Have you ever seen the smile in the eyes of a bird?—the doctor asked.

—No. I've never paid attention to those details. I'm not a meticulous person, as you know. If you ask me about a single grave, what I see is a cemetery.

HE WAS ON THE RUN AND HURTING

He was on the run and hurting. Drowsy with sleep. He wasn't headed anywhere in particular. He was walking among yellow sunflowers that gave way, opening a breach under the purple shadow of the sky.

He saw the evening star born before his eyes. He felt the wind swirl around him. The same wind that pushed the clouds along tearing them apart. He heard the earth moan from the pressure of his footsteps. And he kept going.

He didn't look back, not wanting to see what was behind him.

He noticed his hand drooping, heavy. The same hand that had held the "38 super" when it went off, spewing faded blue bolts of lightning into the midday sun. A cold sweat hung beneath his arms. It extended down to his waist where it made a circle around him.

The sunflowers wilted as the sun went away. He walked through tall stocks of reed grass as the dew began to fall. Then he heard the wailing of the children. A sobbing that surrounded him as if it were fog. Because he had reached the place of fog, where the night watches over the clouds.

The children. That handful of children of the father whom he had just killed.

He felt a shiver. Then he continued on his way. He stopped

when he got to the trees and looked down below, toward the plain, and saw way off in the distance the town that he had left behind.

After the "incident" he tried to avoid his own thoughts. He adjusted his pace in such a way that his mind wasn't free to mull things over. He filled it with noises, with sounds, even with the weeping of the children he had left beside the door while their father was being drilled full of holes. While that man they called "papá" was being nailed to the soft, whitewashed adobe wall with lead spikes. He watched him fall just as dead men fall, with hands open and a bloodied mouth biting into the ground. He heard his teeth resonate as they broke from a mouth that received the full weight of a body stripped of strength and life.

He fled town amid a shower of screams, but with the "38 super" still in his hand, the grip made of seashell sliding in his hand as if it were sweating glass and with his finger dripping as it remained clenched on the trigger.

He had arrived at midday, waiting for the siesta, that time of day when the village would be empty, when everyone is under their own roofs, ruminating or biding their time for the afternoon sun to tumble in. He even thought that he might have to wake him from his siesta. But he was there, watching the kids play. His eyes engrossed in their games.

Those same eyes were delighted to see him. He even raised a hand in salutation. But the other guy responded with a few brilliant lights that burned, all in such quick succession that he wasn't able to grasp what was going on. And when the light went out, even though the sun was still in the sky, he dropped to the ground, headlong, fully and totally, and let go of the last of his strength... Without pain.

—No, I didn't feel any pain—that's what he would have said had someone asked. And if he were still able to answer.

The children screamed. Yes. He heard their screams. And all the windows in town opened and heads emerged in unison. Out of the doorways came bodies that ran towards him, shaking their fists. He saw the commotion and racket that closed around him.

And yet now he was on the run. Directionless. He crossed fields full of sunflowers. And well after dusk he watched as the evening star was born.

He had waited many years for this. He had washed dishes and laundered dirty shirts and underwear on a ship. He had left out of shame, after learning that Carmela, his sister, had been raped. When he went to protest, instead of apologies he received a whipping that left his blood riled from that moment on.

His name was Hermenegildo. His sister's was Carmela. They had been born together, in the same bundle, and both had been orphaned at the same time, at thirteen years of age. And it was about then, more or less, that she gave birth to a son.

The moon was bright that night. The soft sound of moaning woke him, followed by a gasping like that of someone who was dying, and then a scream, protracted and rhythmic like a howl. All taking place on the same night, in little more than an instant.

He beat her until she told him who it had been. Then he took to the street to look for him.

He returned in a bad way, barely able to walk. He wobbled as he entered the house and, completely spent, fell stretched out across the floor. That's how he woke up, his humbled eyes seeing the ground so close up that they couldn't make anything out.

And he left town.

Everyone forgot about him.

Carmela surely had had more children, since he saw a good handful when he closed in on Aniceto to make good on the retaliation he had sworn to deliver.

And he had promised himself, in turn, to save the last shots for himself. And that's what he imagined he had done. After firing toward the front, he shot back on himself, in equal measure: four in that direction, four back this way.

But now he was on the run. He felt the "38 super" that he bought using all his savings cutting into his hand that was stiff and trembling as if it had seized on him. He felt it still trembling, heated by the flames of the burning bullets. Still warm... Warm.

And then came the night. His eyes couldn't see anything but the night. He sat down to rest.

He thought that now was a good time to head back to town to collect his sister and her children. He was determined this time to not abandon his sister or to leave the kids orphaned. "They'll have cried all they can and will be asleep by now."

So he headed back. He crossed the same fields full of sunflowers and entered town. He approached the house along solitary streets flooded with light, and, when he got to the adobe wall next to the door, he dropped his eyes and saw the dead man laid out on the walkway, face down, just as he had been when he fell.

He rubbed his eyes with his hand that was numb from the weight of the pistol and noticed how the midday light was beginning to return. He heard gasping coming from his own mouth and saw people poking their heads through open windows while a din of voices and people running toward him with their fists shaking was encircling him.

But something thick and sticky had once again darkened his sight, and now he couldn't see nor could he hear, and he only had enough strength left to vomit out his own blood.

ÁNGEL PINZÓN PAUSED

Ángel Pinzón paused in the middle where the road to Ozumacín connected with a narrow opening that took him out to his ranch of "Las Vírgenes." He combed the horse's mane and threw his sombrero back as if to let people know who he was, just in case, since his instincts, quite pronounced after years and years of vigilance and waiting, were telling him that at least four or six or perhaps more men were waiting to pounce on him in that very spot. He didn't see anyone, but he could almost feel their breathing. Besides, he expected that it would happen sooner or later, and if not there, then in any other place. What he couldn't understand was the reason they had waited so long, since even the colt seemed irritated, gesturing and circling around on itself, clearly wanting to set off toward its watering holes.

Finally, Ángel Pinzón stood on the stirrups and shouted for all to hear: "Let's get this over with, you *hijos de su mal dormir*! I only ask that you not shoot at my head! And to hell with the mother of anyone who does! You all hear me!

The bullets came immediately from several directions. Striking him in the back and the sides, none in the front; with none hitting the colt that, frightened, ran straight for the opening in the wall as if by instinct it was trying to get away from the hail of bullets.

And that's how, still frantic, it arrived at the entrance to "Las Vírgenes," with its *patrón* still on top, shot full of holes, but still clinging to life.

The Pinzón sisters crowded around the horse. They undid the straps of the saddle that Ángel Pinzón had used to tie around his waist and slowly lowered him, with a carefulness that gave them hope that they might heal his wounds; but twenty holes just can't be fixed. Thus there wasn't anything left to do but to sob. "Don't cry," he told them. "It was my time. I just wanted to appear before God with my face intact." He then dropped his head and rested his soul.

That's how Ángel Pinzón died, next to his sisters, the Pinzonas, to whom their father had left the "Las Vírgenes" ranch so that, when he was gone, they would have something to live off without having to ask anything of anyone. It was a well cared for property that was fed by the water of two rivers that kept the ground moist and it was situated in a large valley full of groves and fruit trees. This left the inhabitants of Ozumacín full of envy since they felt that those lands had been unfairly acquired.

Whether they had been fairly or unfairly gotten is still to be seen. And this is where the story should have begun. Don Tránsito Pinzón, who had had five children, or in other words, Ángel, Engracia, Paz, Inés, and Socorro, never killed anyone, nor did he ever rape a woman, with the exception, of course, of his wife. He lived, as it seemed, a peaceful and quiet life in Ozumacín.

Ozumacín, as you're all aware, lies at the base of Cuasimulco, a high mountain whose summit is covered nearly year round by clouds or by fog. That's why some people believe it to be the place where lightening is born and where thunder resides. No one dares penetrate its cliffs and ravines. And it just so happens that right in front of and not far from Cuasimulco stands Cerro Rabón, another mountain that's said to be the place where tempests dwell. Whether true or not, that's how things are and it's not easy to change people's beliefs.

Cuasimulco faces the east full on and, because of that placement, Ozumacín, located at its base, endures, in exchange for a dawn that lasts forever, a violent dusk and a precipitous night, as if someone had taken a knife to lop off a good-sized chunk of the day. Because of that, whether in summer or in winter, you have to turn your lights on a bit after five in the afternoon.

This caused a bit of anxiety a few years back when people still used candles, especially for business owners, since there was always some delinquent or groups of delinquents who would take advantage of the situation to loot or to steal something.

That's how Don Tránsito Pinzón became a widower, when Don Procopio Argote, who was as blind as a bat, confused Doña Ángela, the wife of Pinzón, with an assailant when he noticed her there in his shop, striking her on the head with a mallet. The thing that worked in Don Procopio's favor was that he had been robbed and beaten the night before by a bunch of thugs from a nearby town.

In those days Ángel Pinzón was coming up on eighteen years of age and his sisters were between twelve and six years old.

Don Tránsito didn't respond by becoming depressed, at least not apparently so. Instead, he was distracted for a few days that were followed by prolonged periods of detachment, until finally, a short time later, he appeared with his son before the notary and, with a large stack of pesos, acquired the "Las Vírgenes" ranch that belonged to none other than Procopio Argote, something that seemed strange to the inhabitants of Ozumacín since Procopio Argote had refused to let go of that property in which so many others had shown an interest.

The explanation came a year later when someone, none other than Ángel Pinzón, discovered his father hanging from a huge ceiba tree next to one of the caves of Cuasimulco. The only mistake the authorities made regarding the dead man was to leave nailed to the ceiba a long list of the names of the men who had asked that this punishment be applied to the thief along with those of the people that he had abducted in exchange for a ransom. Among the names was that of Procopio Argote.

Procopio Argote was Ángel Pinzón's first victim. And if his father, Tránsito Pinzón, had never killed anyone, as he mentioned to the mob that seized him and strung him up, nor had he ever raped anyone, etcetera, etcetera…, Ángel Pinzón searched and searched for several years to find each one of those who had accused his progenitor and then to take their lives. He did just that wherever he found them, going from town to town, from one city to the next, and even having the nerve to go into Ozumacín, unarmed, on the back of his spotted mare that became irritated when he tied it to a pilaster at the entrance and calmly came in to buy provisions to take back to the "Las Vírgenes" ranch.

The people, upon seeing him, ran away frightened or peeked out at him through the lace curtains covering their windows; but nobody dared to greet him or much less to speak to him, although he acknowledged everyone by raising his hand to his sombrero.

The only person he visited was the Tax Collector with whom, after paying his taxes, he carried on a long conversation. He even showed up on one occasion with an injured leg. From then on he limped and even found it difficult to support himself on his lame leg while getting on his mare.

I learned about his exploits in those backwaters through the tax guy and, to tell you the truth, this is where the story of Ángel Pinzón should begin rather than on the day he died; but, oh well, one tells the events of a story in the order they come out and not as one would want.

For example, our tax collector didn't credit Pinzón with quite so many deaths or with all of those that people "reckoned" he was responsible for. That's the word that he used. Later he added: "Common folk are ignorant and are fascinated by the notorious. They're just afraid of Pinzón. They're cowards. That's what they are. If he were a real killer or an up-and-coming one, and he went around advertising it, some lowlife would take him out in an ambush. You see, ever since I was a young man and moved to this miserable little town, there hasn't been a Sunday go by without some dead guy being carted away after a stupid bar fight. On top of that, they think they're somebody: during the week you see dozens of them taking in the sun along the sidewalk, when they should be plowing the ground or working on the fences that are about to fall down around their houses, or going after moles, or fighting one of the many infestations that have ravaged the moun-tainside. But no, they prefer to steal. They've taken two typewriters from me to swap them for a case of beer. Those same bartenders have come by to strike a deal: they'll give me the typewriter back if I pay off the case of beer that they exchanged for it. *Sí señor*, everyone here comes together to screw his neighbor. And now they're panicked over Pinzón, who doesn't even carry a weapon, because they say he's killed a whole bunch of people. *Sí señor*, this town's full of thugs and good-for-nothings."

—And does Ángel Pinzón trust you?

—He does, yes. And I would accuse him of being an assassin as well if there weren't a few factors here and there to soften my thinking.

—Like what?

—Well there's the situation with his sister Engracia who wanted to flee with some guy whose last name I don't even know. As you might not be aware, the father implored Ángel to take care of his sisters. Engracia made it all too easy for that guy to steal her away. So Ángel went after them. He found them that night on the mountain and that's where he gave him what he had coming.

—Just like that?

—I would have done the same thing, especially when we're talking about the older sister who's responsible for the ranch and for the care of the other women.

—It's said that he's always away from "Las Vírgenes," going after those that double-crossed his father. And that he kills them without mercy.

—Perhaps. Anything's possible. He's only mentioned three of them to me. It seems they were all rich folk, but it all happened a long ways from here. I know about a guy from Caborca, that's far away, quite far away. And about another one over by San Ildefonso, but who knows.

—And what can you tell me about what happened to Etelbina, the other sister?

—Well, it turns out that what happened to Etelbina is similar to that of Engracia. She didn't ask for her brother's permission to take a boyfriend and one day he found her at a dance in a town called Copala, two hours from here. He roughed her up as he threw her out, but then really went after whoever that guy was. When that other guy injured his leg, Ángel killed him just like that.

—The dead are piling up, right?

—No, hold up so I can tell the rest of the story. Don't think I'm defending him or trying to minimize the situation. If you think he's evil, he is. Nor am I saying he's a good person. *No señor*, life is corrosive, and after what happened to his father, among other things, well, one's soul can turn bad. In my opinion, Ángel is vile, and he knows it. And he knows he won't die in his sleep; but when his time comes, I'm sure he won't stand in the way. He doesn't understand compassion, nor has he ever heard anyone speak of it. You see, what I can never forgive him for, nor will anyone else, is what he did to the husband of Socorro, his youngest sister.

The three sisters begged their brother to let Socorro get married. They told him how good Miguel was for her. He was about to finish a degree in engineering and whatnot. Finally he agreed and even offered to be the best man at the wedding. He arranged for the church and hired musicians. Everything was in order. The church was overflowing since finally here was something that might erase all that had happened in the past. Everyone left happy.

—*Gracias* Ángel, brother, for what you're doing for Socorro and for us, the three older sisters said.

Ángel not only looked content, but even offered to accompany the bride and groom to the edge of Ozumacín. He traveled at their side mounted on his ruddy mare, but just outside of town he fell back a bit.

—Well brother-in-law, here's where we say goodbye. And without saying another word, he pulled out his pistol and emptied it into Miguel's back. She dropped from the horse to attend to her husband, but there wasn't anything that could be done.

—Mount up and let's get back to "Las Vírgenes." That'll always be your place, right beside your sisters.

If you pass by there, you'll see all four of them, as if they were men: some turning the earth behind a yoke, another feeding the animals, and the oldest in the kitchen, rushing to get dinner on.

This may seem unlikely, but it's true. All of the women who live over at "Las Vírgenes" remain virgins to this day.

THE DISCOVERER

When I met him his name was Candelario José. Years later he showed up with the name of Candelario Lepe because, according to him, he was no longer an *Indio*. While in prison he learned how to read and write and a bit about the law. Perhaps a lot about the law, since through a fair amount of arguing and with a small book titled *Mexicans, This is Your Constitution* that he always carried in his pocket, he devoted himself to getting dozens of his old buddies out of jail. He carried around a bunch of cards with his name and the title of "legal advisor," some of which he gave to me to distribute among my friends. And even though I told him that perhaps none of my friends would need his services, he looked at me earnestly, smiled showing off all the gold of his teeth, and with a slap on the shoulders and his *tejano* hat under his arm, he turned and bounded off. That was in the middle of July of '68. And who would have imagined that three months later I would be looking for him with a long list of people, a list that included my three kids, begging him to arrange their release as soon as possible.

—Please oh please—he said to me—. You get me a certificate and I'll take care of all the arrangements.

—What type of certificate?—I asked.

—A document certified by a Notary Public that I'm no longer an *Indio*.

—That type of document doesn't exist—I said.

—But they can be found—he avowed.

—No, nobody offers a certificate of that nature. It's not necessary. If you feel that you're not an *Indio*, then you're no longer an *Indio*, and that's that. And if that's not the case, then tell me, which tribe do you belong to? To the *Pelos Parados*, or perhaps to the *Patas Prietas*, or which one?

—No—he said—. I was a *Meco*.

—*Meco*... *Meco*, what do you mean by *Meco*?

—*Guachichil*. From the *Guachichil* or *Chichimeco* community.

—Don't mess with me! The *Guachichiles* disappeared from this country at least four hundred years ago, and it's pretty much the same with the *Chichimecas*.

—Well you're wrong. Back home in Juchipila everyone called me and my relatives *meco* sons of this or *meco* sons of that. I heard that up until I was thrown in jail. And I learned a lot in there, but you can't erase my past or the humiliating world in which I lived with my brothers, my parents, and my grandparents. I'm absolutely certain that if I return to Juchipila some day that people will start calling me *Meco* again. That's why I need a legally binding document to rub in their faces and accuse them of defamation if they come back with their crap.

—Look here, Candelario Lepe, you're making things difficult, and you're just looking for something to complicate your life. Someone said, I don't remember who, that "to be an *indio*" you need to feel like an *indio*, live like an *indio*, dress like an *indio*, and think like an *indio*, etcetera, etcetera." I don't see what your problem is.

—Well the issue is perfectly clear to me. I want to go back to Juchipila and be treated like a rational person, just as I am. Or am I not?

—Yes, that's what you are.

—And to be treated like a respectable person, or am I not? Answer me.

—Well, I don't know what the difference is.

—How can you not know what the difference is?

—Look over here—he said, while he put his hands together and had me place mine next to his.

—Now tell me—he told me— what's the difference?

—That's not important at all.

—How can it not be, damn it! Come on, what do you see?

—Some fingernails that are longer than the others—I told him—. And yours are more polished than mine.

—That's from the manicure; but I'm talking about the color of the hands. Go ahead, say something.

—And what do you want me to say? I only see four hands and that's it.

—Don't be a *pendejo*. I want you to tell me which color is darker, but I want you to be the one to point it out.

—No—I told him—.You can get mad at me.That's what you're after, some excuse to throw something in my face. That I'm a racist or something to that effect.

—Do you see? The issue of race came up right away and from there it's all too easy to say that I have the hands of a dark-skinned *indio*, you see?

—Listen to me, Candelario; let's stop this discussion that's going nowhere. I'm going to leave you the list of boys that have been detained to see what you can do to get them free as soon as possible.

Candelario Lepe, with his *tejano* hat always under his arm, took the sheet that was single-spaced and with two columns. He took his time reading the names listed there as if that had some meaning. After a good while he said:

—These are just names.

—All of them were in the Attorney General's office yesterday. They might still be there, but I want you to do something before they move them to Lecumberri prison. You say that you're good at this type of trouble.

—What have they been accused of?

—Of all sorts of things: disturbing the peace, resisting lawful authority, sedition, inciting disorder, and they're saying something about an attempt to overthrow the government. All of that and more; you know how they can pile on offenses when they want to charge someone.

—Yes, but there's not someone here, they're a lot of someones. Let's see, let's put them in order: who are they and what do they do for a living? Or to simplify things, who's likely to be held most responsible? Because you see, from a constitutional standpoint, you can't charge thirty people for doing the same thing. You follow me, right? Some people are doers and others simply follow. How can we personalize these people here? Because this is about people, right? If there were charges on them we could simply separate them. So if they file charges the situation gets easier.

I'm an expert on separating cases. But oh well, leave the report with me and let's see what can be done.

—I'd appreciate it a lot. And look here, these three in the middle are my kids, I hope you can move them to the front.

—Don't worry. I'll try to give them priority.

—So we'll see you later, Candelario. I'll call you tomorrow to see if you have any good news to give me.

I left him while he was still reading the report of those who had been detained as if he were working on some crossword puzzle. He had a scowl on his face and was using a pen to scratch his head. I stopped a taxi on the corner. When we came back up on Candelario I asked him if I couldn't take him somewhere and, without saying yes or no, he opened the door and got into the vehicle.

GLOSSARY OF GENERAL TERMS

AGUARDIENTE: Like brandy, *aguardiente* is a strong alcoholic beverage produced by fermentation and distillation of any variety of local agricultural products.

AMIGO: Friend. "Mi amigo" is "my friend."

ANIMALITO: Diminutive and endearing variation of "animal."

BRAVA LEY: Literally, "Fierce Law" (or fierce temperament). Rulfo explains in his novel that gamecocks designated as *Brava Ley* are "quick to attack."

BRISCA: A card game played using Spanish playing cards.

BRUJA: Witch.

CANELA(S): A hot drink made from water and *canela*, or cinnamon, with alcohol often added.

CANTINA: A tavern or bar.

CAPONERA: See "La Caponera."

CENTAVO: The Mexican peso is divided into one hundred centavos.

CENTEOCÍHUATL: As described in "Castillo de Teayo," Centeocíhuatl is the Huasteca "goddess of germination and rain."

CERVEZA: Beer.

CHACHINITA: Expression of endearment, in the feminine form, that Rulfo uses in "A Letter to Clara."

CHARRO: A traditional Mexican cowboy known for his elaborate clothing, including a large Mexican sombrero, or extra-wide brimmed hat.

CHAYOTE: Originally native to Mesoamerica, the chayote is an edible plant, roughly pear-shaped, belonging to the gourd family, such as melons and squash.

CHICHIMECO (OR CHICHIMECA): See "Guachichil."

COMADRE (OR COMADRITA): Typically used to mean the godmother of one's child, although often employed colloquially to mean friend or neighbor, as in "A Piece of the Night." See also, "compadre".

COMPADRE: Typically used to mean the godfather of one's child. In "A Piece of the Night", the term refers to a close male friend; or, in the plural (*compadres*) to the drunken parents of the child that the protagonist is caring for. See also, "comadre".

CONQUIÁN: A Rummy-style card game that is played using Spanish playing cards.

CORRIDO: A traditional musical style, popular especially in rural areas of Mexico. *Corridos* are ballads that narrate a story, often highlighting the struggles and romances of everyday life.

DON/DOÑA: Title of respect used for men (Don) and women (Doña) who enjoy a significant standing (wealth, influence, or esteem) within the community.

ENCHILADA(S): A Mexican dish that consists of rolled tortillas that are filled with some ingredient such as meat or cheese and topped with a chile-based sauce.

GOLPE DE GRACIA: *Coup de grâce*, or death blow.

GRACIAS: Thanks.

GUACHICHIL(ES): An indigenous people that belonged to the pre-Columbian Chichimeco (also Chichimeca or Chichimec) nation. The Guachichiles occupied an extensive area that included portions of the central Mexican states of Zacatecas, San Luis Potosí, Guanajuato, and Jalisco. A character of "The Discoverer" claims to be descendent from the Guachichiles or Chichimecos based upon the harassing that his family receives from local townsfolk who call them "mecos," short for Chichimeco.

HACIENDA: A large country estate.

HECHO EL TIRO: Literally, "the shot is made." Expression within the novel that the croupier uses to indicate that the ball of the roulette table has been put in play.

HIJOS DE SU MAL DORMIR!: A colloquial variation on the expletive "Sons of bitches."

HUASTECA/HUASTECOS: Huasteca is the indigenous name of a significant region of Mexico that includes parts of the states of Veracruz, Hidalgo, San Luis Potosí, and Tamaulipas. The indigenous inhabitants of this region, speakers of one of the many Mayan languages, are known as Huastecos.

IMBÉCIL(ES): Idiot(s).

INDIO: Indian. As in English, the term connects to a long and difficult history of racial discrimination and can have negative connotations. Such is the case in "The Discoverer" where Rulfo presents a character, Candelario Lepe, who is obsessed with freeing himself of the injurious associations of the designation.

LA CAPONERA: Nickname given to Bernarda Cutiño. Literally, "lead mare," or a mare that is used to guide and coax a number of other horses.

LA PINZONA. Nickname given to Bernarda Pinzón. The label is a play both on the nickname of the girl's mother, *La Caponera* (with "la" being the feminine article in Spanish), and on the last name that she took from her father, Dionisio Pinzón. The younger Bernarda is also called Bernardita, or "little Bernarda."

LAS VÍRGENES: Name of a fictitious ranch in "Ángel Pinzón Paused," that means, literally, "The Virgins."

LEY SUPREMA: Literally "Supreme Law" (or extraordinary temperament). Rulfo explains in his novel that gamecocks designated as "Ley Suprema" are "persistent fighters who throw solid jabs and display courage up to last moments of their lives."

LICENCIADO: Licentiate, a title given to someone who has earned a particular university degree. In the novel, there are two brothers who claim to have degrees as lawyers who are referred to as *licenciados*.

MALILLA: A type of card game using Spanish playing cards.

MAMÁ: Mother, or mom.

MARIACHI(S): A traditional form of Mexican folk music. The term is also used to refer to the members of a mariachi band. Mariachi bands typically include several musicians, all dressed in *charro* style, playing a variety of instruments, including violins, trumpets, and guitars.

MAYECITA: A term of endearment that Rulfo uses in "A Letter for Clara."

MECO: See "Guachichil."

MEXICA: The Mexica (or Mexicas) are commonly known today as the Aztecs. Originally a nomadic tribe, the Mexica settled in central Mexico in the 13th century and established their capital, Tenochtitlán, in 1325. When Hernan Cortez arrived in 1519, the Aztecs were the dominant empire of the region. The Spaniards built their own capital, Mexico City, on the ruins of Tenochtitlán.

MEZCAL (OR MESCAL): A strong alcoholic beverage similar to tequila that is made from the maguey plant.

MIRASOL CHILE: A type of hot pepper, red in color and popular in Mexico that, when dried, is known as the guajillo chile.

MOCHILLER: A cockfighting term that, as Rulfo explains in his novel, refers to the first cockerel to be fought and that is considered to be the best.

MUCHACHO(S): Boy(s). *Mis muchachos,* or "my boys," is used in the novel by *La Caponera* to refer to the members of her mariachi band.

NAVEGANTES: Literally, "navigators." The term refers to a few slices of prickly pear cactus leaves floating in a bowl filled mostly with broth, a meal that reflects the impoverished condition of Dionisio Pinzón.

NO SEÑOR: No sir.

PACO GRANDE: Or simply *Paco.* A card game that uses Spanish playing cards.

PADRINO: A patron or protector. In the context of cockfighting, a *padrino* is a person who guarantees the bets made on behalf of a particular rooster.

PALAPA: An open-air structure that is covered with a thatched roof made typically from dried palm leaves.

PAPÁ: Father, or dad.

PATAS PRIETAS: See "Pelos Parados."

PATRÓN: Boss, an employer or superior.

PELOS PARADOS: One of the characters of "The Discoverer" challenges his friend by asking, in a derisive manner, if he's still an *indio,* to which tribe does he belong: "To the *Pelos Parados,* or perhaps to the *Patas Prietas,* or which one?" The friend's mockery is heightened by the fact that he seems to be naming, in an inexact fashion, two tribes that are found in the United States and Canada rather than in Mexico: the *Pelos Parados* (literally "Standing Hair", or perhaps the Mohawks, with their unique hairstyle) and the *Patas Prietas* (likely a reference to the Blackfoot nation).

PENDEJO: A soft expletive that refers to someone who is stupid and that might be translated as "dumbass" in English.

PESO: The Mexican monetary unit.

PETATE: A rectangular mat woven from plant fibers. Although a part of

Mexican culture since pre-Colombian times, the contemporary use of a *petate* for sleeping is likely to be associated with individuals of indigenous and/or impoverished backgrounds.

PEONES: Literally "peons," unskilled laborers.

PINZONA: See "La Pinzona."

PISTOLERO(S): Gunman(men) or hired gun(s).

PITAYA (or Pitahaya): The fruit of several cactus species. In one of *La Caponera*'s songs, she mentions the white flower of the pitaya that grows on the tree-like garambullo cactus plant.

¡POBRECITA DE MÍ!: Poor me! Said by Cleotilde as an exclamation after she receives a fatal beating by her husband ("Cleotilde").

POLÍTICO(S): Politician(s).

POTRERO HONDO: Literally, the "bottom pasture." Used in the novel as a proper noun.

PRESIDENTE MUNICIPAL: Municipal president, or the government official in charge of leading a municipality. See the note on municipalities at the beginning of the glossary dedicated to geographical names.

PUEBLO: Town.

PULQUE: A traditional alcoholic drink made from the fermented juice of the maguey plant.

QUIEBRANUECES: Literally, "nut cracker." The term appears in "A Piece of the Night" as a reference to the pimp for whom Pilar works. Rulfo's interesting and disparaging use of this compound word suggests both the violent and sexual nature of his protagonist's initiation into the world of prostitution.

RANCHO, OR RANCHITO: A ranch, with "ranchito" being the diminutive form.

REBOZO: A traditional shawl that, more so in previous generations, was commonly worn by women in Mexico, especially in rural areas.

REQUESÓN: A Mexican cheese fairly similar to Ricotta cheese.

SEÑOR(ES) / SEÑORA(S): A title or form of address, similar to "Sir" or "Mr." for men (*señor*) or "Ma'am" or "Mrs." for women (*señora*). The masculine plural (*señores*) is also used when both men and women are addressed together.

SÍ SEÑOR: Yes sir.

SIESTA: A period of rest during the hottest part of the day, often observed in Hispanic communities of Spain and Spanish America where it is desirable to escape the heat of the early afternoon.

SIETE Y MEDIO: A card game that uses Spanish playing cards.

SOMBRERO: A traditional oversized Mexican wide-brimmed hat.

TAMALE: English spelling taken from the plural of *tamal* (i.e. *talmales*). A traditional Mexican dish made of a corn-based dough (or *masa*) that is wrapped and steamed in a large banana leaf or corn husk.

TEJANA HAT: Similar to the western-style cowboy hat of the United States, a *tejana* is made of high quality felt or animal skin and is likely much more expensive than the sombreros worn by other characters of *The Golden Cockerel*.

TEOCALI (or teocalli): Teocalli is a Nahuatl word (the language of the Aztecs) that refers to a pyramid that includes some form of temple, or sacred space, on top.

TEQUILA: A traditional alcoholic beverage made from the maguey plant. The drink is typically produced in the central Mexican regions (especially the state of Jalisco) where *The Golden Cockerel* is centered.

TOLOLOCHE: A traditional Mexican string instrument that produces low notes similar to the double bass.

TORTERÍA: A shop that sells *tortas*, or Mexican-style sandwiches.

TOTONACO (or Totonac): The Totonaco lived in eastern Mexico and were subject to the Aztec Empire prior to the arrival of the Spanish in 1519. As described in "Castillo de Teayo," the Totonacos were often at war with the Huasteca people.

TU MUCHACHO: You're boy. Signature used by Rulfo in a letter he wrote to Clara.

VAMOS (or VÁMONOS): Let's go. This expression appears in the text as an exclamation, which, in Spanish, includes an inverted exclamation point preceding the word: *¡Vamos!*

VÍRGENES: See "Las Vírgenes."

VIVA: Part of a cheer in support of a person, place, or idea, as in "*¡Viva Quitupan!*" ("Long live Quitupan").

ZOPILOTE MOJADO: Literally, "The Wet Buzzard," a traditional Mexican mariachi song.

GLOSSARY OF GEOGRAPHICAL NAMES

NOTE ON MUNICIPALITIES: The Mexican Republic is divided into thirty-one states and one capital city with importance similar to that of a state (Mexico City, abbreviated as CDMX). Each state is divided into municipalities that are roughly equivalent to counties in the United States. One city or town (called a *localidad*, or locality) within each municipality serves as the *cabecera municipal*, or seat of the municipal government. Many states and municipalities in Mexico share the name of a significant locality. Chihuahua, for example, is the name of the state, of the municipality within the state, and of a major city. In *The Golden Cockerel* (and sometimes in his other writings) it can be assumed that Rulfo is most frequently referring to the locality or to the state, although the distinction is not always clear.

AGUASCALIENTES: Capital of the state of Aguascalientes in central Mexico. The city was founded in 1575 and is home to the famous San Marcos Fair.

ALTOS, LOS: Los Altos, meaning "the highlands," refers to the northeastern region of the state of Jalisco. Los Altos is mentioned in Rulfo's synopsis of *The Golden Cockerel*, but not in the novel itself.

AJUSCO: A high lava dome volcano situated just south of Mexico City. Rulfo, who was an avid alpinist, mentions wanting to climb Ajusco in his "A Letter to Clara."

ÁLAMO: Town in the state of Veracruz named for the many poplar or "álamo" trees along the nearby Pantepec River.

ARANDAS: Town in the Los Altos region along the eastern side of the state of Jalisco and seat of the municipality of the same name.

ÁRBOL GRANDE: Likely a small village or community in the state of Jalisco. When Dionisio asks about Bernarda Cutiño who abandoned him in Santa Gertrudis (located in Jalisco), Colmenero Secundio indicates that he last saw her in a place not far away called Árbol Grande.

BAJÍO: The Bajío (literally lowlands) is a fertile agricultural region in central Mexico that includes portions of the states of Guanajuato, Querétaro, Aguascalientes, and Jalisco.

CABORCA: Mentioned in "Ángel Pinzón Paused" as being a long ways away, Caborca likely refers to a small city in northern Mexico, in the state of Sonora.

CASTILLO DE TEAYO: A Mesoamerican archaeological site located in the Huasteca region of Mexico in the northern part of the state of Veracruz that was occupied around the 10th to 12th centuries. Castillo de Teayo can refer to the contemporary settlement that has grown up around the archeological site, to the site itself, or to the main pyramid or "castle" (castillo) that dominates the location. In his fictionalized travelogue titled "Castillo de Teayo," Rulfo refers primarily to the pyramid itself.

CELAYA: City in the state of Guanajuato. The area has a strong connection to the history of the Mexican Revolution since it was in Celaya in 1915 that the troops of Francisco "Pancho" Villa were defeated by Álvaro Obregón, forecasting the eventual demise of Villa's revolutionary efforts.

CEMPOALA: The Totonac capital located in the contemporary state of Veracruz, Cempoala was defeated by Aztec warriors in the middle of the fifteenth century.

CERRO RABÓN: A mountain in northern Oaxaca state that forms part of the Sierra Madre Oriental range.

CHALCHICOMULA: Chalchicomula de Sesma is a municipality in the state of Puebla. The municipal seat is located in Ciudad Serdán, previously known as San Andrés Chalchicomula.

CHAVINDA: A small, high-altitude town in the Mexican state of Michoacán. Chavinda is mentioned in Rulfo's synopsis of *The Golden Cockerel*, but not in the novel itself.

CHICONTEPEC: Chicontepec de Tejeda is a town that is also the seat of the Chicontepec municipality, located in the state of Veracruz.

CHIHUAHUA: Capital of the state by the same name. The state of Chihuahua is the largest of the Mexican Republic and is located in north central Mexico, sharing a long border with portions of the American states of New Mexico and Texas.

COCOTLÁN: Small town in the northern part of the state of Jalisco.

COPALA: Mentioned in "Ángel Pinzón Paused," San Juan Copala is a small town in the state of Oaxaca.

CUASIMULCO: As described in "Ángel Pinzón Paused," Cuasimulco is "a high mountain with its crest covered in clouds nearly year round." Cuasimulco is located in the Chinantec indigenous region of northern Oaxaca state.

CUQUÍO: Town in the state of Jalisco and seat of the municipality by the same name.

HUASTECA/HUASTECOS: See Glossary of General Terms.

JARDÍN DE SANTIAGO: The Santiago Garden mentioned in "A Piece of the Night." Rulfo is referring to the Jardín de Santiago Tlatelolco, located in the Guerrero neighborhood of Mexico City just off the Paseo de la Reforma, one of the capital's main avenues. The garden is a bit north of the Plaza de Garibaldi, about two kilometers from

Valerio Trujano Street where Pilar, the prostitute protagonist of this story, typically works the night.

JUCHIPILA: A municipality in the state of Zacatecas.

LECUMBERRI PRISON: Also known as the Palacio de Lecumberri, this large building in Mexico City served as a penitentiary from 1900 to 1976 and was often used to hold political prisoners.

LOS ALTOS: See "Altos, Los."

MATA OSCURA: A small town in northern Veracruz.

NOCHISTLÁN: Town in the state of Zacatecas and seat of the municipality of Nochistlán de Mejía.

OGAZÓN STREET. Mentioned in "A Piece of the Night" as perhaps the farthest point that the protagonists reach during their late night wanderings through Mexico City. The street is about 3.5 kilometers from Valerio Trujano, although the pair seem to be wandering in a less than straight line.

OZUMACÍN: San Pedro Ozumacín is a small town in northern Oaxaca state where a large percentage of the inhabitants speak the indigenous Chinantec language.

PAPANTLA: City and municipality located in the north of the state of Veracruz, an area considered to be a tropical rainforest.

PINOS: Town and seat of the municipality by the same name located in the state of Zacatecas. Pinos is located in a region known for its mining.

PLAZA DE LOS ÁNGELES: Mentioned in "A Piece of the Night," this plaza is located just off of Lerdo Street, slightly south of the Tlatelolco Archeological site.

POPO: Popo (or Popocatépetl) is an active volcano that is situated just outside of Mexico City. Rulfo, who was an avid alpinist, mentions wanting to climb (or "say hello to") the Popo in his "A Letter to Clara."

POZA RICA: A city and municipality in northern Verazcruz state.

QUITUPAN: Town in the state of Jalisco and seat of the municipality by the same name.

RINCÓN DE ROMOS: A city in the state of Aguascalientes. Rincón de Romos is mentioned in Rulfo's synopsis of *The Golden Cockerel*, but not in the novel itself.

SAN JUAN DEL RÍO: Town in the state of Querétaro and seat of the municipality by the same name.

SAN JUAN SIN AGUA: Small town in the state of San Luis Potosí whose name literally means "Saint John Without Water." San Juan Sin Agua is mentioned in Rulfo's synopsis of *The Golden Cockerel*, but not in the novel itself.

SAN LUIS POTOSÍ: Founded in 1592, San Luis Potosí is the capital of the state bearing the same name.

SAN MARCOS FAIR: An important fair held every year in the state of Aguascalientes. The activities last for about three weeks around the date of April 25, the Feast Day of San Marcos.

SAN MIGUEL DEL MILAGRO: The hometown of Dionisio Pinzón. The symbolic and biblical qualities of the name (literally, Saint Michael of the Miracle) likely appealed to Rulfo whose interest in the metaphoric qualities of place names can be seen clearly in *Pedro Páramo* (e.g. Comala and La Media Luna). The actual town of San Miguel del Milagro is located in the state of Tlaxcala, near the archeological site of Cacaxtla. Despite its small size (currently just over 1,100 inhabitants), the town has been, and remains, an important pilgrimage site for many faithful Catholics, who believe that Saint Michael appeared there in 1631.

SANTA GERTRUDIS: A small settlement in the municipality of Tonaya in the state of Jalisco, not far from where Juan Rulfo spent his early childhood. In *The Golden Cockerel*, Santa Gertrudis is the name both of this small settlement and the large hacienda owned first by Lorenzo Benavides and later by Dionisio Pinzón. Sergio López Mena suggests that Rulfo may have taken an actual hacienda in Santa Gertrudis that forms the "nucleus" of the community as the inspiration for the oversized and underused shell of a home that is such an important part of the second half of Rulfo's novel (*Diccionario de la obra de Juan Rulfo*. Mexico City: UNAM, 2007. p. 202).

SAN ILDEFONSO: Small town mentioned in "Ángel Pinzón Paused" that likely refers to San Ildefonso Villa Alta in the state of Oaxaca.

TABUCO: Location along the coast in the northern part of the state of Veracruz.

TAPAMANCHOCO: Location "at the edge of the lagoon" where, as Rulfo describes in "Castillo de Teayo," lies the burial ground of the lost warriors."

TEAYO: See Castillo de Teayo.

TEOCALTICHE: Town in the state of Jalisco and municipality by the same name.

TEQUISQUIAPAN: Town in the state of Querétaro and municipality by the same name.

TIHUATLÁN: A municipality in northern Veracruz state.

TLAQUEPAQUE: Important city in the state of Jalisco and municipality by the same name. Known also as San Pedro de Tlaquepaque.

TUXPAN: City and municipality located in the state of Veracruz that is mentioned in "Castillo de Teayo" as a pre-Colombian population center.

VALERIO TRUJANO STREET: Named after a hero of the War of Independence, Valerio Trujano is a short roadway that runs north from the Alameda in Mexico City and connects with the Paseo de la

Reforma. Its location, just off of the Alameda, an impressive urban park and one of the capital city's main gathering places, would make it a desirable spot for the prostitute protagonist of "A Piece of the Night." Indeed, that street and surrounding areas were known as places where women could ply the "oldest profession" in the decade of the 1940s in which the story is likely set. Furthermore, Rulfo gives enough detail for the reader to follow the late-night wanderings of his protagonists. From Valerio Trujano street they head northeast toward the Garibaldi and Tlatelolco neighborhoods of Mexico City, stopping at the Jardín de Santiago, making it as far north as Ogazón Street, before headed back toward the Plaza de los Ángeles.

VERACRUZ: Mexican state that enjoys a long coastline along the Gulf of Mexico. The state's capital of Veracruz was originally founded in 1519 by Hernan Cortez before heading inland to the Aztec capital of Tenochtitlan.

ZACATECAS: Capital of the state by the same name. Founded in 1548, Zacatecas was, during the Colonial period, an important mining region.

JUAN RULFO: A CHRONOLOGY

1876-1911

The "**Porfiriato**," or those years in which the dictator **Porfirio Díaz** governs in Mexico.

1910-1917

The Mexican Revolution, often considered the nation's most important political and social event of the twentieth century. Armed resistance to the government of Porfirio Díaz begins officially on November 20, 1910. Although Díaz flees the country in early 1911, fighting will continue for several years. A new constitution is adopted in 1917 by the government of **Venustiano Carranza** and many consider this date the official end of the Revolution, although significant and often violent opposition to the new regime in Mexico City will continue.

1917

Juan Rulfo is born on May 16 in Sayula in the state of Jalisco.

1919

Emiliano Zapata, an important and iconic general of the Mexican Revolution, is assassinated.

The Rulfo family moves to San Gabriel, a small town in the state of Jalisco.

1920

Venustiano Carranza is assassinated and **Álvaro Obregón** becomes Mexico's new president.

1923

Rulfo's father, known by the nickname **Cheno**, is murdered on June 1.

Francisco "Pancho" Villa who had been a major participant in the Revolution in northern Mexico is assassinated on July 20.

1926-1928

The Cristiada, or Cristero War, an uprising against the oppressive anti-clericalism of the post-Revolution government of **Plutarco Elías Calles**. The Cristero War proves to be particularly violent, with much of the fighting centered in and around Rulfo's home state of Jalisco.

1927

Rulfo and his older brother **Severiano** move to Guadalajara to attend a boarding school.

Rulfo's mother, **María**, passes away at the end of the year.

1933-1936

Travels between Guadalajara and Mexico City. His attempts to earn an advanced degree, first at the University of Guadalajara and then at the National University (UNAM) in Mexico City, prove difficult for various reasons, including lengthy student strikes.

1934–1940

Presidency of **Lázaro Cárdenas**, a leader known for his policies of land reform and the nationalization of the oil industry.

1936

Begins working in various capacities for the government's Secretariat of the Interior (Secretaría de Gobernación), including as a migration agent.

1945

Publishes three stories in periodicals: "Life Doesn't Take Itself Very Seriously" ("La vida no es muy seria en sus cosas"), "They Have Given Us the Land" ("Nos han dado la tierra"), and "Macario." He will publish a few additional stories sporadically before the release of *The Plain in Flames* (*El Llano en llamas*) in 1953.

1947–1952

Begins working for the international tire company Goodrich Euzkadi.

1948

Marries **Clara Aparicio Reyes**.

1949

Publishes his photography for the first time in the magazine *América* (number 59, February).

1952–1953

Receives a scholarship from the **Centro Mexicano de Escritores**

(Mexican Writing Center) that funds Rulfo's creative efforts.

1953

Publishes *The Plain in Flames* (*El Llano en llamas*).

1953-1954

Receives his second scholarship from the Centro Mexicano de Escritores.

1955

In March, publishes *Pedro Páramo*.

In November, works as an historical advisor on the set of the *The Hidden One* (*La Escondida*), a film set during the Mexican Revolution and directed by **Roberto Gavaldón**.

1956

It is likely that Rulfo begins to write *The Golden Cockerel* (*El gallo de oro*) in 1956, perhaps finishing the project during the following year.

1959

Works with **Antonio Reynoso** to shoot *The Spoils* (*El despojo*), a short film based on a text by Rulfo.

1962

Begins working at the **National Indigenist Institute** (Instituto Nacional Indigenista), a federal organization created in 1948 to acknowledge the nation's indigenous heritage and to improve the lives of its native peoples. Rulfo would work in the Publications Department for the remainder of his life.

1964

Premier of the film **The Golden Cockerel** (*El gallo de oro*), directed by **Roberto Gavaldón**, an adaptation of Rulfo's second novel.

Rubén Gámez films **The Secret Formula** (*La fórmula secreta*), including a voice-over reading of a text by Juan Rulfo. The following year the film would win first place in the *Primer Concurso de Cine Experimental*, a competition organized to promote experimentation in the Mexican film culture.

1966

The first adaptation of **Pedro Páramo** is filmed (appearing in early 1967), directed by **Carlos Velo**.

1968

The Massacre of the Plaza of Tlatelolco, a mostly student-led demonstration in the Tlatelolco neighborhood of Mexico City, ends when military forces fire on the crowd. Only ten days later Mexico City hosts the **Summer Olympic Games**.

1970

Rulfo receives Mexico's **National Literary Prize**.

1976

Pedro Páramo: The Man from The Media Luna (*Pedro Páramo: El hombre de La Media Luna*) the second film adaptation of Rulfo's first novel is completed (and premiers in 1977), directed by **José Bolaños**.

1980

An **Homenaje Nacional**, or national celebration in honor of Juan Rulfo is hosted in the Palace of Fine Arts in Mexico City. The event includes an exhibition of the author's photography that results in the first major publication of his visual production, titled *Juan Rulfo: Homenaje nacional*.

A second book of Rulfo's photography is published as *Inframundo: El México de Juan Rulfo*. Rulfo's photographic production would begin to appear frequently in print and in exhibitions starting about a decade after the author's passing in 1986.

The Golden Cockerel is published for the first time as *El gallo de oro y otros textos para cine*. Rulfo seems to have had little say in the release of this text.

1983

Rulfo receives the **Prince of Asturias Literary Award** in Spain.

1986

Juan Rulfo dies from a heart attack on January 7 at his home in Mexico City.

Filming of *The Realm of Fortune* (*El imperio de la fortuna*), the second film adaptation of *The Golden Cockerel*, directed by Alberto Ripstein. It is released in 1987.

JUAN RULFO (1917–1986) was one of Mexico's premier authors of the twentieth century and an important precursor to the Latin American literary "Boom" in the 1960s that included such prominent writers as Gabriel García Márquez, Mario Vargas Llosa, and Carlos Fuentes. Rulfo's first novel, *Pedro Páramo* (1955), and his short story collection, *The Burning Plain* (1953) are considered among the best and most influential works of twentieth century Latin American narrative fiction. In addition to his literary works, Rulfo was a photographer and worked for a short time as a writer for film. Rulfo received Mexico's National Prize for Literature (Premio Nacional de Literatura) in 1970, was elected to the Mexican Academy of Language (Academia Mexicana de la Lengua) in 1980, and received the Cervantes Prize (Premio Cervantes), the highest literary award in Spanish, in 1985. Rulfo suffered from lung cancer in his final months and died on January 7, 1986 at his home in Mexico City.

DOUGLAS J. WEATHERFORD earned a PhD in Hispanic Literature from the Pennsylvania State University in 1997 and is currently a professor in the Department of Spanish and Portuguese at Brigham Young University (Provo, Utah). He has developed teaching and research interests in a wide range of areas related to Latin American literature and film, with particular emphasis on Mexico during the mid-twentieth century. Much of his recent scholarship has examined Mexican author Juan Rulfo's connection to the visual image in film. Additionally, Weatherford was the faculty curator of a 2006 exhibit of Rulfo's photography titled "Photographing Silence: Juan Rulfo's Mexico" (Museum of Art, Brigham Young University).

Thank you all
for your support.
We do this for you,
and could not do
it without you.

DEEP
VELLUM

DEAR READERS,

DeepVellum Publishing is a 501c3 nonprofit literary arts organization founded in 2013 with a threefold mission: to publish international literature in English translation; to foster the art and craft of translation; and to build a more vibrant book culture in Dallas and beyond. We are dedicated to broadening cultural connections across the English-reading world by connecting readers, in new and creative ways, with the work of international authors. We strive for diversity in publishing authors from various languages, viewpoints, genders, sexual orientations, countries, continents, and literary styles, whose works provide lasting cultural value and build bridges with foreign cultures while expanding our understanding of how the world thinks, feels, and experiences the human condition.

Operating as a nonprofit means that we rely on the generosity of tax-deductible donations from individual donors, cultural organizations, government institutions, and foundations. Your donations provide the basis of our operational budget as we seek out and publish exciting literary works from around the globe and build a vibrant and active literary arts community both locally and within the global society. Deep Vellum offers multiple donor levels, including LIGA DE ORO ($5,000+) and LIGA DEL SIGLO ($1,000+). Donors at various levels receive personalized benefits for their donations, including books and DeepVellum merchandise, invitations to special events, and recognition in each book and on our website.

In addition to donations, we rely on subscriptions from readers like you to provide an invaluable ongoing investment in Deep Vellum that demonstrates a commitment to our editorial vision and mission. Subscribers are the bedrock of our support as we grow the readership for these amazing works of literature from every corner of the world. The investment our subscribers make allows us to demonstrate to potential donors and bookstores alike the support and demand for Deep Vellum's literature across a broad readership and gives us the ability to grow our mission in ever-new, ever-innovative ways.

In partnership with our sister company and bookstore, DeepVellum Books, located in the historic cultural district of Deep Ellum in central Dallas, we organize and host literary programming such as author readings, translator workshops, creative writing classes, spoken word performances, and interdisciplinary arts events for writers, translators, and artists from across the globe. Our goal is to enrich and connect the world through the power of the written and spoken word, and we have been recognized for our efforts by being named one of the "Five Small Presses Changing the Face of the Industry" by *Flavorwire* and honored as Dallas's Best Publisher by *D Magazine*.

If you would like to get involved with DeepVellum as a donor, subscriber, or volunteer, please contact us at deepvellum.org. We would love to hear from you.

Thank you all. Enjoy reading.
Will Evans Founder & Publisher Deep Vellum Publishing

LIGA DE ORO ($5,000+)

Anonymous (2)

LIGA DEL SIGLO ($1,000+)

Allred Capital Management
Ben & Sharon Fountain
David Tomlinson & Kathryn Berry
Judy Pollock
Life in Deep Ellum
Loretta Siciliano
Lori Feathers
Mary Ann Thompson-Frenk
& Joshua Frenk
Matthew Rittmayer
Meriwether Evans
Pixel and Texel
Nick Storch
Social Venture Partners Dallas
Stephen Bullock

DONORS

Adam Rekerdres
Alan Shockley
Amrit Dhir
Anonymous (4)
Andrew Yorke
Anthony Messenger
Bob Appel
Bob & Katherine Penn
Brandon Childress
Brandon Kennedy
Caitlin Baker
Caroline Casey
Charles Dee Mitchell

Charley Mitcherson
Cheryl Thompson
Christie Tull
CS Maynard
Cullen Schaar
Daniel J. Hale
Deborah Johnson
Dori Boone-Costantino
Ed Nawotka
Elizabeth Gillette
Rev. Elizabeth
    & Neil Moseley
Ester & Matt Harrison

Farley Houston
Garth Hallberg
Grace Kenney
Greg McConeghy
Jeff Waxman
JJ Italiano
Justin Childress
Kay Cattarulla
Kelly Falconer
Lea Courington
Leigh Ann Pike
Linda Nell Evans
Lissa Dunlay

Marian Schwartz
& Reid Minot
Mark Haber
Mary Cline
Maynard Thomson
Michael Reklis
Mike Kaminsky
Mokhtar Ramadan
Nikki & Dennis Gibson

Olga Kislova
Patrick Kukucka
Patrick Kutcher
Richard Meyer
Sherry Perry
Steve Bullock
Suejean Kim
Susan Carp
Susan Ernst

Stephen Harding
Symphonic Source
Theater Jones
Thomas DiPiero
Tim Perttula
Tony Thomson

SUBSCRIBERS

Ali Bolcakan
Amanda Harvey
Amanda Watson
Marta Habet
Anthony Brown
Ben Fountain
Ben Nichols
Ben Nichols
Blair Bullock
Chris Sweet
Christine Gettings
Christie Tull
Courtney Sheedy
David Christensen
David Tomlinson
& Kathryn Berry
David Travis

David Weinberger
Elaine Corwin
Farley Houston
Frank Garrett
Ghassan Fergiani
Heath & Martina Dollar
Horatiu Matei
James Tierney
Jeanne Milazzo
Jeffrey Collins
Jeremy Strick
Joe Milazzo
Joel Garza
John O'Neill
John Winkelman
Kimberly Alexander
Kristin Porter

Margaret Terwey
Martha Gifford
Matthew Lovitt
Michael Elliott
Neal Chuang
Nhan Ho
Nicola Molinaro
Patrick Shirak
Peter McCambridge
Rainer Schulte
Steven Kornajcik
Suzanne Fischer
Tim Kindseth
Tom Bowden
Tony Messenger
Tracy Shapley
Whitney Leader-Picone

AVAILABLE NOW FROM DEEP VELLUM

MICHÈLE AUDIN · *One Hundred Twenty-One Days*
translated by Christiana Hills · FRANCE

CARMEN BOULLOSA · *Texas: The Great Theft* · *Before* · *Heavens on Earth*
translated by Samantha Schnee · Peter Bush · Shelby Vincent · MEXICO

LEILA S. CHUDORI · *Home*
translated by John H. McGlynn · INDONESIA

ANANDA DEVI · *Eve Out of Her Ruins*
translated by Jeffrey Zuckerman · MAURITIUS

ALISA GANIEVA · *The Mountain and the Wall*
translated by Carol Apollonio · RUSSIA

ANNE GARRÉTA · *Sphinx* · *Not One Day*
translated by Emma Ramadan · FRANCE

JÓN GNARR · *The Indian* · *The Pirate* · *The Outlaw*
translated by Lytton Smith· ICELAND

NOEMI JAFFE · *What are the Blind Men Dreaming?*
translated by Julia Sanches & Ellen Elias-Bursac · BRAZIL

CLAUDIA SALAZAR JIMÉNEZ · *Blood of the Dawn*
translated by Elizabeth Bryer · PERU

JOSEFINE KLOUGART · *Of Darkness*
translated by Martin Aitken · DENMARK

YANICK LAHENS · *Moonbath*
translated by Emily Gogolak · HAITI

JUNG YOUNG MOON · *Vaseline Buddha*
translated by Yewon Jung · SOUTH KOREA

FOUAD LAROUI · *The Curious Case of Dassoukine's Trousers*
translated by Emma Ramadan · MOROCCO

LINA MERUANE · *Seeing Red*
translated by Megan McDowell · CHILE

FISTON MWANZA MUJILA · *Tram 83*
translated by Roland Glasser · DEMOCRATIC REPUBLIC OF CONGO

ILJA LEONARD PFEIJFFER · *La Superba*
translated by Michele Hutchison · NETHERLANDS